I'LL SELL YOU A DOG

I'LL SELL YOU A DOG

Juan Pablo Villalobos

Translated by Rosalind Harvey

LOS ANGELES · HIGH WYCOMBE

First published in English translation in 2016 by
And Other Stories
High Wycombe – Los Angeles
www.andotherstories.org

Lines by James Hillman were reprinted with permission from *The Dream and the
Underworld* (HarperCollins Publishers, 1979) and *Re-Visioning Psychology* (HarperCollins
Publishers, 1992). Lines by Francisco de Quevedo were taken from *Dreams and
Discourses*, translated by RK Britton (Aris and Phillips). Lines from the Bible were
taken from the authorised King James Version (Oxford University Press). Lines from
Theodor Adorno's *Aesthetic Theory* were reprinted with permission from translations
by Robert Hullot-Kentor (Bloomsbury, 2013). Lines from Adorno's *Notes to Literature*
were reprinted with permission from the translation by Shierry Weber Nicholsen
(Copyright © Columbia University Press, 1993). Lines by Marcel Proust were taken
from CK Scott Moncrieff's translation, *Remembrance of Things Past* (Chatto & Windus).
Lines from Juan O'Gorman's interviews in *La luz de México* by Cristina Pacheco (Estado
de Guanajato), Daniel Sada's *Registro de causantes* (Planeta) and from Silvio Rodríguez'
song 'Al final de este viaje en la vida' (Ojalá Records) were translated by Rosalind
Harvey. Permission has been sought from all rightsholders.

ISBN 9781908276742
eBook ISBN 9781908276759

Editor: Sophie Lewis; copy-editor: Tara Tobler; proofreader: Laura Willett; typesetter:
Tetragon, London; typefaces: Linotype Swift Neue and Verlag; cover design: Elisa
von Randow.

This book has been selected to receive financial assistance from English PEN's PEN
Translates programme, supported by Arts Council England. English PEN exists to
promote literature and our understanding of it, to uphold writers' freedoms around
the world, to campaign against the persecution and imprisonment of writers for
stating their views, and to promote the friendly co-operation of writers and the free
exchange of ideas. www.englishpen.org

CONTENTS

For Andreia

Her pink dress unsettles me. It won't let me die.

JUAN O'GORMAN

Perhaps I'll understand in the next life;
in this one I can only imagine.

DANIEL SADA

There isn't a stomach that wouldn't howl with hunger
if all the dogs you've thrust down them were
suddenly brought back to life!

FRANCISCO DE QUEVEDO

AESTHETIC THEORY

In those days, as I left my apartment each morning, number 3-C, I would bump into my neighbour from 3-D in the hall, who had got it into her head that I was writing a novel. My neighbour was called Francesca, and I, it goes without saying, was not writing a novel at all. You had to pronounce her name *Frrrancesca*, really rolling the 'r's, so it sounded extra trashy. After greeting each other with a raise of the eyebrows, we'd stand and wait in front of the doors to the lift, which divided the building in two, ascending and descending like the zip on a pair of trousers. It was comparisons like this that made Francesca go around telling everyone else who lived in the building that I was forever coming on to her. And because I called her Francesca, which wasn't her real name but the name I'd given her in this so-called novel of mine.

There were days when the lift would take hours to arrive, as if it didn't know the people using it were old and assumed we had all the time in the world ahead of us, as opposed to behind. Or as if it did know, but couldn't care less. When the doors finally opened, we'd get in and begin the agonisingly slow descent, and the colour would begin to rise in Francesca's face purely from the effect of the metaphor. The contraption moved so slowly it seemed it was being operated by a pair of mischievous hands that were taking their time on purpose so as to enhance the arousal and delay the consummation, when the zip finally reached the bottom. The cockroaches infesting the building would take advantage of our trip and travel downstairs to visit their associates. I used the dead time in the lift to squash a few of them. It was easier to chase after them in there than at home, in the corridors or down in the lobby, although it was more dangerous, too. You had to step on them firmly but not too hard, or else you ran the risk of the elevator plummeting sharply down from the force. I told Francesca to stand still. Once, I stamped on her toe and she made me pay for her to get a taxi to the podiatrist.

Waiting for her in the lobby were her minions, the poor things: she ran a literary salon in which she forced residents to read one novel after another. They spent hours down there, her 'salonists', as they called themselves, from Monday through to Sunday. They'd purchased some little battery-powered lights – Made in China – from the street market, which they clipped to the front covers of their books together with a magnifying glass, and looked after them with a care so obscene you'd think they were the most important invention since gunpowder or Maoism. I slunk through the chairs, arranged in a circle like in rehab or a satanic sect, and when I reached the main door and sensed the proximity of the street with its potholes and stench of fried food, I shouted a goodbye to them:

'Lend me the book when you've finished! I've got a table with a wonky leg!'

And without fail, Francesca would reply:

'*Francesca* sounds like an Italian prostitute, you dirty old man!'

The literary salon had ten members, plus the chair. From time to time one would die or be declared unable to live unassisted and move to a home, but Francesca always managed to hoodwink the new resident into joining up. Our building consisted of twelve apartments arranged over three floors, four on each storey. It was widowers and bachelors who lived there, or rather I should say widows and spinsters, because women made up the majority. The building was at number 78 Calle Basilia Franco, a street like any other in Mexico City, by which I mean as filthy and flaking as any other. The only anomaly on it was this place, this ghetto of the third age, the *little old people's building* as the rest of the neighbourhood called it, as decrepit and shabby as its inhabitants. The number on the building was the same as my age, the only difference being that the numbering on the block didn't increase with every year that passed.

Proof the salon was actually a sect lay in the fact that they spent such a long time on those chairs. They were folding aluminium chairs, bearing the logo of Corona beer. I'm talking about literary fundamentalists here, people capable of convincing the brewery's marketing manager to give them chairs as part of their cultural sponsorship programme. As unlikely as it seems, the subliminal advertising worked: I would leave the building and head straight for the bar on the corner, for the first beer of the day.

The salon wasn't the only blot on the building's weekly routine. Hipólita, from 2-C, imparted classes in bread-dough modelling on Tuesdays, Thursdays and Saturdays. Then there was an instructor who came on Mondays and Fridays to do aerobics classes round the corner, in the Jardín de Epicuro, a park filled with bushes and shrubs and where there were more nitrogen and sulphur oxides, more carbon dioxide and monoxide than oxygen. Francesca, who had been a language teacher, gave private English lessons. And then there were classes in yoga, IT and macramé, all organised by the residents themselves, who seemed to think retirement was like preschool. You had to put up with all of this as well as the lamentable state of the building, but the rent had been frozen since the beginning of time, which made up for it.

Trips to museums and places of historical interest were also organised. Every time someone stuck a leaflet up in the lobby about an excursion to some exhibition, I would jab a finger at it and ask:

'Anyone know how much beer costs in this dump?'

It wasn't an idle question: I'd paid as much as fifty pesos for a beer in a museum café once. The price of a month's rent! I couldn't afford that kind of luxury; I had to survive on my savings, which, according to my calculations, would last another eight years at this rate. Long enough, I thought, before old lady death came to pay me a visit. *This rate*, by the way, was what they called *a stoic life*, although I called it a crappy life, plain and simple. I had to keep track of the number of beers I had each day so as not to go over budget! And I did keep track, methodically – the problem was that I lost track come the evening. So those eight years were perhaps miscalculated and were only seven or six. Or five. The thought that the sum of drinks I had each day might go into subtraction and end up becoming a countdown made me pretty nervous. And the more nervous I was, the harder I found it to keep track.

At other times, as the lift descended, Francesca would start giving me advice on writing the novel which, like I said before, I wasn't writing. Going down three floors at that speed gave her time to cover two centuries of literary theory. She said my characters lacked depth, as if they were holes. And that my style needed more texture, as if she were buying fabric to make curtains. She spoke with astonishing clarity, articulating each syllable so carefully that no matter how outrageous the ideas she put forward they sounded like gospel. It was as if she reached the absolute truth via correct pronunciation and employed hypnosis techniques on top of that. And it worked! This was how she had come to be dictator of the salon, chair of the Residents' Association, the ultimate authority on the subject of gossip and slander. I stopped paying attention and would close my eyes to concentrate on the descent of my fly. Then the lift would give a jolt as it reached the lobby and Francesca knitted together one final phrase, whose loose end I clutched at, having lost the thread of her rant:

'You're as bad as the Yucatecs, who have the same word for searching and finding.'

And I would reply:

'If you do not seek, you will not find.'

This was a phrase of Schoenberg's that reminded me of my mother seventy years earlier, when I had lost a sock. I searched and searched and then it turned out that the dog had eaten the sock. My mother died in 1985, in the earthquake. The dog beat her to it by over forty years and in his haste he never discovered how the Second World War ended: he swallowed a pair of nylon tights, incredibly long ones, as long as my father's secretary's legs.

I'd come to live in the building one summer afternoon a year and a half ago, carrying a suitcase with some clothes, two boxes of belongings, a painting and an easel. The removal company had brought the furniture and a few appliances that morning. As I crossed the lobby, dodging the bulky forms that made up the salon, I repeated:

'Don't trouble yourselves, don't trouble yourselves.'

Of course, no one did trouble themselves and they all just pretended to carry on reading, although what they were actually doing was looking sidelong at me. When I finally got to the lift doors, I heard the rumour that began on Francesca's lips and spread from mouth to ear like a party game:

'He's a painter!'

'He's a waiter!'

'He's a baker!

'He's a Quaker!'

I took everything I could fit up in the lift and, ten minutes later, as I returned to the lobby to carry the rest up, like an oh-so-slow Sisyphus, I found that the salonists had organised a cocktail party to welcome me with fizz from the state of Zacatecas and savoury crackers spread with fish paste and mayonnaise.

'Welcome!' Hipólita shouted, handing me a bottle of DDT spray. 'It's just a little something, but you'll need it.'

'You must forgive us,' said Francesca, 'we didn't realise you were an artist! We would have put the champagne on ice if we'd known.'

I took the plastic cup she handed me, full to the brim with warm fizzy wine, and held out my arm to make a toast when Francesca exclaimed:

'To art!'

I'd extended my arm a little too horizontally, so instead of making a toast it looked like I was trying to give them the cup back, which was, in fact, what I wanted to do. They then asked me to speak, to say a few words in the name of art, and what I said, peering sadly at the furious bubbling coming from the disposable cup, was:

'I'd prefer a beer.'

Francesca took a crumpled twenty-peso note from her purse and ordered one of her minions:

'Go to the shop on the corner and get the artist a beer.'

Somewhat bewildered, I just managed to head off the jumble of questions trooping towards me in an attempt to dispel my anonymity:

'Excuse me but how old are you?'

'Are you a widower?'

'What's wrong with your nose?'

'Where did you live before?'

'Are you a bachelor?'

'Why don't you brush your hair?'

I stood stock-still and smiled, my cup of fizz untouched in my right hand, the DDT spray in my left, until there was a silence when I could reply.

'So?' Francesca said.

'I think there's been a misunderstanding,' I said, unfortunately before the guy who was going to fetch the beers had left the building. 'I'm not an artist.'

'I told you! He's a baker!' Hipólita shouted triumphantly, and I noticed her mouth was crowned with a fine dark fuzz of hairs.

'Actually, I'm retired,' I continued.

'A retired artist!' Francesca crowed. 'No need to apologise, we're all retired here. All of us except those who never did anything.'

'I retired, from my family,' Hipólita chipped in.

'No, no, I was never an artist,' I assured them so vehemently even I was suspicious.

One of the salon members who was heading over to offer me a plate of crackers stopped in his tracks and put it down on one of the chairs.

'Shall I get the beer or not?' the other minion called from the doorway.

'Wait,' Francesca ordered, then asked me: 'What about the easel and the painting?'

'They were my father's,' I replied. 'He liked to paint. I used to like painting too, but that was a long time ago.'

'Just what we need, a frustrated artist!' Francesca exclaimed. 'And from a long line of them, too! May I ask what you used to do?'

'I was a taco seller.'

'A taco seller?'

'Yeah, I had a taco stand in the Candelaria de los Patos.'

The salon members started pouring the fizzy wine back into the bottle and, since their hands were shaking, half the liquid spilled onto the floor. Francesca looked over at the man awaiting the denouement in the doorway and commanded him:

'Give me the twenty pesos.'

I felt the weight of the cup in my right hand disappear, felt Hipólita grab the DDT spray from my left hand, watched Francesca's minion return the crumpled note to her and the entire salon pull the plug on the cocktail party, handing out the remaining crackers and putting the cork back in the bottle before taking up their books again. Francesca still stood there, looking me up and down, down and up, etching my shabby figure onto her mind's eye, before declaring:

'Impostor!'

I looked closely at her too, taking in her figure, her long, svelte, rake-like body, noticing that she had let down her hair and undone the first few buttons at the front of her dress while I'd been going up and down in the lift, felt the rare twinge in my crotch and, realising pretty quickly what she was about, gave the first of many shouts that, from that day forth, would be the catchphrase of our shtick:

'Well, I beg your pardon for having been a taco seller, *Madame!*'

My mother had demanded an autopsy for the dog and Dad was attempting, fruitlessly, to prevent it.

'What use is it knowing what the dog died of?' he asked.

'We have to know what happened,' my mother replied. 'Everything has an explanation.'

The creature had spent the previous night trying to be sick, without success. Mum counted the socks: every pair was complete. This is when she became suspicious, because my father used to take the dog out for a walk every day after dinner. She paid the butcher to slit the animal open. They carried the carcass out to the little patio in the back where we hung out the washing and which my mother had carpeted with newspapers. While the preparations went on, Dad followed my mother around, saying over and over:

'Is this necessary? Is it really necessary? Poor animal, it's barbaric.'

I tried to calm him down:

'Don't worry, Dad, he can't feel anything any more.'

I was about to turn eight at the time. The preparations continued and, instead of trying to halt the operation, my father promised to paint a portrait of the dog that they could hang in the living room, so Mum would never forget him.

'A figurative portrait,' Dad hastened to add; 'none of that avant-garde stuff.'

My mother didn't even reply to such a proposition. There was an outstanding, that is to say, never-ending dispute over a cubist portrait of Mum my father had painted when they were courting and which he had given her as a wedding present. She hated the picture because, depending on the mood she was in, she said it made her look like a clown, a monster or a deformed whale.

'Is it really necessary?' my father asked again.

'I don't want it to happen again and to stop it from happening again we have to know what happened,' my mother explained.

A child of eight could have drawn his own conclusions, because it couldn't happen again. The dog couldn't die twice. My sister, who was a year older than me but maturing as fast as a papaya, took me into a corner and said:

'Look at Dad's face: he looks like he's the one whose guts they're going to cut open.'

My father was the colour of the sheets on my bed, which although old and worn were pretty white still, thanks to the gallons of bleach my mother used. The butcher asked if my father was going to faint, if he was scared of blood. It was a very warm summer evening and it would be wise to hurry up, before the dog began to stink. With the regal sangfroid typical of her whenever she was settling a family dispute, my mother replied:

'You may proceed.'

The butcher made a cut from chin to belly. The blood ran out onto a photo of President Ávila Camacho, his hands raised as if being attacked, although presumably he was actually being applauded. Mum bent down to peer into the dog's entrails, like some Etruscan mystic trying to see the future – and she did see it, quite literally, because the future is always a fateful consequence of the past. An endless nylon stocking had coiled itself along the entire length of the dog's intestines. It was like what Schoenberg said, but backwards, which meant the same in the end: my mother had found her explanation. Dad protested, claiming the dog had been sniffing around downtown, near Alameda Central park. My parents' house was also in a neighbourhood in the centre.

'The doghouse is too good for you,' said my mother.

I laughed and my father gave me a slap. My sister laughed and my mother pinched her arm. We both began to cry. By dinner time, Dad could take it no longer: with no excuse to go out, he simply left and never came home again. The butcher had taken the dog's corpse away and promised to bury it. My sister had followed him and told me she'd seen him cutting a deal with the taco vendor on the corner. She also told me not to tell our mother, because she'd been very fond of the dog. This is what she spent her life doing, growing fond of dogs.

The next day, Mum was so upset she didn't feel like making dinner. To conceal this from us, she took us out for tacos. She said it was the start of a new life. My sister said that if that was the case then she'd rather have *pozole* for dinner. I fancied enchiladas. It was impossible to change her mind – tacos were the cheapest option. When the taco seller saw us heading for his stand he shook his head like we were depraved. It wasn't as if it was unheard of. Weren't there people who grew fond of their chickens and then cooked them in mole sauce, and on their birthday of all things?

24

Several theories about the origins of my novel had occurred to me. What I mean is, about how Francesca had got it into her head that I was writing a novel. The most logical thing would be to blame it all on how ridiculously thin the walls in the building were, practically imaginary, which led to the immense popularity of espionage as a recreational activity. But she must also enjoy telling tales and be harbouring some kind of hidden agenda. Otherwise what was the point of going around telling everyone I was writing a novel if I wasn't writing one?

I had a few notebooks I used to scribble in, that at least was true, especially late at night, as I let the last beer of the day slide down my throat, a beer which sometimes became the second-to-last. Or the third-to-last. I would draw and write down things that occurred to me. I drew and wrote and gradually nodded off, until the pen slipped from my hand and I slipped over towards my bed. But between this and writing a novel there was a huge stretch, an abyss that could only be crossed with a great deal of will power and naivety. Where had Francesca got the idea that what I was writing in my notebook was a novel?

What really intrigued me was how the woman had managed to find out the contents of my notebook, because her knowledge of what was in it was eerily detailed, and she would recount it to everyone who attended her salon as if it was the new chapter in a long-running serial. I played up to this and began sending her messages. Beneath a drawing of a male dog mounting a little female, I wrote in my shaky hand like a long-legged spider:

> *Francesca – I'll wait for you tomorrow in my apartment, at 9 p.m. I'll pop a pill at half past eight so we'll have plenty of time to have a couple of beers and get to know each other. Let me know if you'd prefer something stronger. Tequila? Mezcal? Or would you rather a whisky? I've got a really good one from Tlalnepantla. Wear something pretty, a leather miniskirt or that red dress you were wearing when we went to see the courtyard at the Colegio de San Ildefonso.*

The next morning, the entire salon was waiting for me down in the entrance hall spoiling for a fight. They began to lob rotten tomatoes at me from the greengrocer's stand outside, clamouring:

'That's no way to write a novel!'

'You dirty old man!'

'That's not a novel!'

And I replied:

'I told you!'

The following day, just to drive them mad, I copied out whole paragraphs from Adorno's *Aesthetic Theory* into my notebook:

> *The demand for complete responsibility on the part of artworks increases the burden of their guilt; therefore this demand is to be*

set in counterpoint with the antithetical demand for irresponsibil-
ity. The latter is reminiscent of the element of play, without which
there is no more possibility of art than of theory . . . A solemn
tone would condemn artworks to ridiculousness, just as would the
gestures of grandeur and might . . . In the artwork the uncondi-
tional surrender of dignity can become an organon of its strength.

Troy burned: they bought two pounds of tomatoes each.

I had acquired the bad habit of trying to resolve all quar-
rels by reciting paragraphs from *Aesthetic Theory*. So far I'd
dispatched more than one telemarketing agent, several street
sellers, dozens of insurance salesmen and someone who
wanted to sell me a plot for my own grave in six instalments.
I'd found my edition in a library funded by the foundation of a
bank four blocks from where I lived. I stuffed the book down
my trousers and underneath my shirt, and arranged my face
to look like I was wearing a colostomy bag. A thief robbing
a thief. On the first page, a blank one, was a stamp from the
faculty of philosophy at the Universidad Nacional Autónoma
de México. A thief robbing a thief robbing a thief. On page
22, without looking, I found the phrase of Schoenberg's that
reminded me of my mother: if you do not seek, you will not
find. My *Aesthetic Theory* had been shoved in between the
memoirs of the gay writer and intellectual Salvador Novo and
Fray Servando, the priest. Schoenberg wouldn't have liked
this, nor would have Adorno, and nor would my mother: if
you do not seek, you can find, too.

And on the third day, when expediency had tempered her disappointment, Francesca knocked at the door to my apartment. It was a very hot day and the neckline of her dress led me to cherish unwonted hopes, as if it were possible to win the Battle of Puebla without actually going to Puebla. She wore her hair down and around her neck hung a slender gold necklace from which, in turn, hung an equally slender ring, apparently an engagement ring.

'May I come in?' she asked.

I stepped aside to let her in and followed this with the mechanical courtesy of telling her to make herself at home. It occurred to me that I should have gone to the pharmacist. I made a mental note: *go to pharmacist.*

'Would you like a beer?' I asked.

'I'd prefer something else,' she replied. 'An anisette. Or an almond liqueur.'

'I've only got beer. Or water.'

'Some water, then.'

'Please, have a seat.'

I went over to get her some water while she sat down in the chair, my only chair, which I'd installed in front of the television. Out of the corner of my eye, I saw her inspect my apartment in detail, pausing when she came to the painting hanging on the opposite wall and the little shelf by the door where I'd piled up all my notebooks and a few other volumes, not a novel among them. There was little else to look at: the little dining table, two boxes I had yet to unpack and – naturally – the cockroaches.

After I'd handed her the water I stood in front of her, leaning against the table because there was nowhere for me to sit, and watched as she took a microscopic sip. The truth was that, my intentions aside, the only place the two of us could have been comfortable was on the bed. I crossed my arms to let her know I was waiting. She waited for a few seconds before speaking, as if first she needed to make sure, in her mind, of the construction of the phrase she was about to enunciate. Finally she opened her mouth, and what she said was: 'I've come to formally invite you to join the literary salon.'

The tune echoed around my head in the moment that followed, as Francesca took another tiny sip of her water: I've *come* to *for*mally in*vite* you to *join* the *li*terary *sa*lon. This pause appeared to be studied so the phrase had time to take effect, so I would have time to come to the conclusion that this was an honour. An undeserved honour, naturally, and – were I to accept – the source of Francesca's power over me from this moment onwards.

'Thank you very much,' I told her, 'but I'm not interested. I don't read novels.'

The glass in her right hand trembled; she'd drunk so little water that she almost spilled it down herself. She directed her gaze to the shelf by the door.

'Those books aren't novels,' I added, to clear up any confusion seeing them from a distance might have occasioned her.

Francesca turned back to me and took another breath to resume her attack, this time employing an unusual strategy.

'But you're writing a novel, and if you want to write a novel the best thing to do is to read, to read a lot.'

'What?!' I said, a reply and a question.

'Yes: you have to be very aware of literary tradition, otherwi—'

'I am not writing a novel; where on earth did you get that idea from?'

'Don't lie, everyone knows everything in this building, we're a very close-knit community.'

'A very nosy one, you mean.'

She flinched in irritation and held out her glass for me to put it down on the table.

'Have you forgiven me for being a taco seller yet?' I said, my voice dripping with sarcasm. 'Do you think a taco seller is fit to write a novel?'

'If you have a good ear, then yes, you must have heard lots of interesting conversations. But it's a long way from listening to writing; if you like I can help, the salon could be very useful for you.'

'That's nice, but I don't read or write novels.'

'Everyone comes to the salon.'

'Not me.'

'The previous tenant did.'

'And that's how he died! You think I don't know what happened to him?'

The previous occupant of my apartment had dropped dead, in the middle of reading Carlos Fuentes' last novel, of a heart attack right out there in the lobby, where a wooden cross had been hung in his memory under the mailboxes, as if Fuentes himself had run him down in a sports car.

'I know you and I have got off on the wrong foot,' said Francesca, leaning forward so that the ring on her necklace dangled in the air and the neckline of her dress revealed another centimetre of cleavage. 'The salon is a chance for us to fix this.'

It seemed to me that the ring on her necklace was spinning around and I was afraid she was trying to hypnotise me.

'There's nothing to fix,' I replied, looking away towards a little patch of sky I could see outside the balcony. 'We're not broken.'

'Excuse me?'

'I mean I don't hold grudges, so never mind.'

'We'll see you tomorrow, then? We start at ten. I've got a copy of the novel we're reading all ready for you. We're only on the second chapter, you'll catch us up in no time. I can give you the previous tenant's little reading light, if you're not morbid about such things?'

'Don't insist, please – I'm not going to come.'

She stood up, brushing a heap of imaginary crumbs from her dress.

'Which doesn't mean that you and I can't be friends,' I continued. 'Come and have a drink with me in the bar on the corner, and on the way I can buy some pills I need – what do you say?'

'You can't write a novel without reading novels!' she declared.

'Perfect! Two birds with one stone!'

She left without responding to my invitation. When I investigated the interest concealed behind her insistence, as well as her political strategies for controlling the building, I discovered a slightly more trivial yet undoubtedly more decisive motive: the bookshop where she ordered the novels gave her a special discount for buying a dozen copies.

Whenever there was an argument at home, my mother would win it by saying that Dad had an *artistic temperament*. Given the tone of voice she used and the context in which she said it, it sounded like a physical defect. In actual fact, it was slander that my father never quite learned how to refute: he tried to do so verbally, but his actions betrayed him, time and again, and the examples my mother stored up to confirm her diagnosis multiplied.

Months before he abandoned us, he had the idea of painting a rotting papaya. He had brought a small, slightly wrinkly one home from the market and had placed it, sliced in half and accompanied by a white carnation in a glass of water, on a table by his easel. He changed the position of the fruit and the angle of the flower several times and, when he was satisfied with the composition, he warned us:

'No one is to touch anything. And don't eat the papaya. My painting will be a study on death, decadence, decay and the finite nature of life.'

Of course, the next day, before the papaya went off and to prevent the proliferation of swarms of mosquitoes fascinated by the composition, my mother cut the papaya into cubes and fed it to me and my sister, while Dad was out. I couldn't bring myself to eat the fruit, so I hid it and gave it to my father when he came back from work. When he reproached my mother for betraying him, she replied: 'If you're going to waste a papaya, you have to have enough money to buy two.'

This was before Dad got his job as a sales manager, where they even gave him a secretary, which turned out to be an advancement with unfortunate consequences for the family. My father held up the plate with the little cubes of papaya in the palm of his hand, surrounded by a halo of mosquitoes, and lamented: 'The boy's the only one who understands me.'

My mother replied: 'You're a terrible example to him. The last thing we need is for him to end up an artist too! Why don't you draw the little cubes of papaya? You can make it a cubist painting. It'll be a study of the incomplete, the fragmentary, the finite nature of the resources of a family whose sole breadwinner spends his time with his head in the clouds, revelling in the frustration caused by his *artistic temperament*.'

Dad gave the papaya back to me.

'You can eat it now,' he said.

But I still couldn't eat it: I hid the plate under my bed and only threw it away when the flies tried to lay their eggs in my ears.

I escaped from the volley of tomatoes as best I could and headed straight for the greengrocer's, where I was greeted with a hearty laugh:

'Good and ripe, were they?' she'd ask. 'I saved the best ones for you, they're from the Hyatt Hotel!'

'You shouldn't give that sanctimonious lot ammunition!' I protested.

'Everyone has the right to rebel, even them!'

The greengrocer had made rebellion her way of life and her principal source of income: I never saw her sell a single vegetable that was in the least bit edible. Instead, she acted as the official supplier to every riot. Her foul-smelling tomatoes were famous at all the well-known sites of demonstration: on Paseo de la Reforma, down in the Zócalo, on Avenida Bucareli; she even furnished the peasants of San Mateo Atenco with vegetables when they rose up to protest at their land being confiscated to build the airport.

The best thing about the greengrocer was that she was five years younger than Francesca and eleven years younger than me. At this stage in life the effect of age difference has to be multiplied by three, at least. One might say that Francesca was better preserved than the greengrocer, which was logical, considering the wear and tear of an intellectual life as opposed to one of action. But the state of preservation didn't matter because we weren't bottles of milk in the refrigerator, or wagons from the 1930s or '40s. What really mattered were the desires and motives Francesca suspected the greengrocer of having, more intense than her own, and far more so in Francesca's head than in reality. Since reality was another thing that didn't matter and what Francesca thought actually did, I calculated that my flirting with the greengrocer could well end up increasing my chances with Francesca. And all this without even taking into account the ostentatious dimensions of the greengrocer's chest! It was a psychological and sexual battle that would have made even Freud's beard stand on end.

On the wall of the vegetable shop was a calendar showing special commemorative dates to observe and the vegetables that were in season on each one. March was the time of the renationalisation of oil reserves, the birth of Benito Juárez, courgettes and chayote. May was high season: Labour Day, the Day of the Holy Cross, the Battle of Puebla, Teachers Day, Students Day, chayote, lettuce and tomato. In September, Poblano chillies, the annual presidential speech, Boy Heroes Day and Independence Day. In October and November there were only a few dates, but more tomatoes than ever were sold: the Tlatelolco Massacre, the Day of the Hispanic Peoples and the Mexican Revolution.

The greengrocer would stretch out a chubby arm and hand me a roll of toilet paper with which to wipe the flecks of tomato from my face, hair, neck and arms, and give me a yellow T-shirt from the 2006 electoral campaign to change into. I would return the T-shirt to her later, only for her to lend it to me again after the next barrage of tomatoes. This happened so often that, in time, people in the street came to think I was a supporter of the Party of the Democratic Revolution. Then she would yell out an order for two big bottles of Superior from the shop on the corner, a girl would bring the beer, and the greengrocer would pour us each a glass and begin:

'So, where did you leave the intellectuals?'

'Back there – they ran out of tomatoes and went back to their little books.'

'And to think how much they're needed out here in – '

Our chats were interrupted by some trucks arriving to unload past-their-best vegetables: from the restaurants and hotels of Polanco, from the branch of Superama on Avenida Horacio, from the Las Américas racetrack; even from a greengrocers up in the fancy neighbourhood of Las Lomas. Instead of throwing the rotting produce away and, above all, to stop the beggars from hanging around their premises to collect it, they had been persuaded to donate it to the greengrocer so she could sell it at 'community prices' to those most in need. This was what she had told them and, in a way, she hadn't lied. In her shop, the price of a pound of tomatoes was one per cent of market price. For the price of one pound of fresh tomatoes, rioters could get a hundred pounds of ammunition. It was a truly community-minded act, although not the one the donors had imagined: they would receive the vegetables that their exquisite palates had rejected smack in the face.

We sipped our beer and by the second glass, without fail, it was Francisco I Madero's turn. Always Madero: the nation's fate had gone downhill because of Madero. Things would have been very different, the greengrocer said, if Flores Magón had led the Revolution instead.

'You know what we should do?' she asked, not waiting for me to answer. 'What we should do is put a few bullets into Madero.'

'They did that already, right there by the Palacio de Lecumberri,' I reminded her.

'Well, let's do it again, then! Do you know where he's buried?'

We made plans to go and desecrate Madero's tomb in the Monument to the Revolution. It was close by, three metro stops away. Along with Madero were buried Pancho Villa and José Venustiano Carranza, Plutarco Elías Calles and Lázaro Cárdenas del Río, all of them sworn enemies. The only thing they had in common was that they all had moustaches. The greengrocer shouted:

'That's what dialectic's for: building monuments!'

Madero had been killed exactly one hundred years ago, in February 1913, but in the greengrocer's head it was as if it had happened yesterday. She lived in a time when all the misfortunes of the nation, from the murder of Zapata to the electoral fraud committed against López Obrador, happened simultaneously, or were placed right up close to each other like a series of rocks encircling the planet and then heading out into space, all the way to Pluto.

The greengrocer had another theory about my novel, or rather about how Francesca knew what was in my notebook. According to this hypothesis, Francesca was a CIA agent. I refused to accept this, because experience had taught me that reality does not bow to ideology.

'Think about it,' she said. 'Do you know anything about her? Whether she's widowed or divorced, whether she's got kids, whether she's a spinster, what she used to do?'

'I know she was a language teacher,' I replied.

'You see! English teachers work for the CIA, everybody knows that. It was even in a film. How do you think she ended up in your building?'

'She entered the draw, like the rest of us.'

'No one ends up there that way. Did you enter a draw to get a place there? Only influential people get an apartment in that building. Skint, but influential.'

Despite the saying that silence speaks volumes, I kept my mouth shut; I didn't like to reveal how I'd got the apartment. You were supposed to fill in a load of forms and pray to every saint under the sun, first for one of the current residents to die or be declared incapable of living unassisted, and then for the bureaucrats to awaken from their superannuated torpor and set the process in motion. On top of this you had to be selected by lottery and the probability of success was one in thousands. Barring the part when the dead resident was carried out, leaving the apartment available, this procedure was never adhered to.

'She came to the building because she's on a mission,' said the greengrocer.

'But she's retired.'

'A CIA agent never retires!' she would repeat. 'Do you think if she was retired she'd need to live in that shabby old place, that stuck-up old thing? If she was retired she'd be living in Tepoztlán or Chapala, somewhere fancy like that. I'm telling you, she's on a mission, that's why she's spying on you and brainwashing everyone in her salon at the same time. Think about it: all she needs is a glass tumbler, she holds it up against the wall and then puts her ear against it.'

'But I don't write out loud!'

'You wouldn't even need to! These people can decipher your writing by listening to the pen scratching away in your notebook.'

She suggested that when I wrote in the book I should use some kind of device that made a noise to foil Francesca's attempts to spy on me. So the next time I grew bored of drawing, I switched on the blender, which I never used, and wrote some things down in my notebook that I'd remembered:

> *Five hundred riot police were sent to capture Alejandro Jodorowsky for crucifying a chicken. José Luis Cuevas painted a temporary mural and invented the Pink Zone. The bones of José Clemente Orozco, Diego Rivera, Dr Atl and Siqueiros ended up in the Rotunda of Illustrious Men. Juan O'Gorman took cyanide, put a rope around his neck and then put a bullet in his brain. His bones ended up in the same place. La Esmeralda art school was moved to the neighbourhood of Colonia Guerrero. One of Rufino Tamayo's paintings was auctioned off for seven million dollars, one of Frida's for five, another of Diego's for three. The Rotunda's name was changed: where it had said 'Men' they changed it to 'Persons'. They moved María Izquierdo's remains to the Rotunda of Illustrious Persons.*

The next morning, Francesca was waiting out in the hallway and when I left my apartment she ran over to confront me.

'That's the last thing we need! Taco sellers who think they're art historians.'

'Do you know what a customer once said to me?' I replied. 'That that was precisely what we needed: taco sellers who knew about art, who were interested in art.'

'Who was your customer? Gorky?'

'If Gorky were alive he'd be shocked at the price of beer in museum cafés.'

I complained to the greengrocer that her theory had failed.

'All I managed to do was blow up my blender.'

'It must be telepathy, then.'

'I knew it! You're mad.'

'That's precisely what the CIA's strategy is – don't you get it? They use crazy techniques so that no one believes it when they are discovered.'

'So what does she get out of spying on me?'

'You should know, you're probably a danger to the system.'

'Yeah, right!'

'Well, I've always thought you were suspicious, you know? All that clowning around's got to be a ploy to distract people. Who knows what secrets you're hiding . . . Or perhaps the future of the human race depends on your notebook, just imagine!'

With the help of a comrade who was undercover, she'd gone so far as to get hold of a list of names of supposed CIA agents in Mexico. We couldn't find Francesca's.

'But that's not her real name!' the greengrocer said.

So we looked for her real name, or at least, the one the salon members called her by, the same one her post was addressed to and with which she signed the minutes of the Residents' Association meetings. That one wasn't on the list, either.

'You see?' I said.

'That only proves one thing: that name's false, too. You really think she's going to use her real name? I'm telling you, she's on a mission! Actually, now I think of it, we shouldn't be using our real names either.'

'What do you want to be called?' I asked her.

41

'I don't know, can you think of a name? Pick a pretty one.'

'What about Juliet?'

'Juliet?'

'Yeah, but pronounced the French way, *Juliette*, so it packs more of a punch.'

'I like it! What about you?'

'I want to be called Teo.'

'Mateo?'

'As if!'

'Well what, then?'

'Teodoro, but just call me Teo.'

You had to say her name *Juliette* to make Francesca jealous. Then Juliet would dare me to force my way into 3-D, Francesca's apartment, to confirm her theory. This usually happened around the third beer, when I would wisely take my leave. I needed to rest a little in order to get through the rest of the day. On my way back from the greengrocer's shop, when I crossed the lobby and looked around at the salon members, all hypnotised by their books, perfectly pacified, I'd call out:

'Still here? How are your piles doing?'

And Francesca would shout:

'*Juliette* is the name of a French whore!'

One morning the salon was cancelled because a poet had died and everyone rushed off to mourn the dead man. Everyone except Hipólita, whose varicose veins prevented such exertion. I was about to shoot off like a rattletrap rocket to the bar on the corner when I ran into her, putting her hand into the letter boxes to deposit a piece of paper: she was organising an exhibition of little birds modelled out of bread dough down in the lobby. I folded up the invitation to the vernissage and put it in my back pocket, and was almost at the door when Hipólita intercepted me.

'You're an ungrateful wretch.'

I turned around to face her. She had come close enough to the entrance that the morning light accentuated the down on her upper lip. Away from the lobby's deceptive gloom it was a proper moustache.

'I don't get a mention in your novel,' she explained.

'You know it's not a novel.'

'You must think I'm so insignificant.'

'My dear, you talk like one of Frida Kahlo's paintings: nothing but moaning. Hey, did you see that?'

I pointed at the right-hand wall of the lobby, covered in damp patches, and then fled as fast as my bunions allowed.

That night I wrote in my journal about a childhood memory: my mother's brother, a bachelor who had been the first taco seller in the family, had a moustache so outrageous he used to get bits of food stuck in it.

'It's a northern thing,' my mother would say, excusing him.

Her family was from San Luis Potosí which, technically speaking, wasn't even in the north. If anything it was the south of the north. I had seen him spend an entire Sunday afternoon with the tail end of a jalapeño pepper entangled in his whiskers.

The next day there were new chairs in the lobby. Reclining wooden ones, with cushioned backs and seats, super comfortable. They'd nicked them from the poet's funeral. These were truly dangerous people: they'd lugged them all the way from Bellas Artes, six stops on the metro. The new chairs didn't fit in the room we used as a dumping ground, where the folded Corona beer chairs were stored. They started leaving the new ones lined up on either side of the lobby, like in a waiting room. The salon members considered them the pinnacle of elegance. The cockroaches rather liked them, too.

Posterity decreed that the dead poet was only mediocre: he failed to merit a statue or even an avenue named after him, never mind a place in the Rotunda of Illustrious Persons. They named a dirt road after him in Irapuato, where he'd been born. Then another poet died (poets were always dying). The salon members seized the opportunity to steal another chair for Hipólita. This poet had a statue erected to him in a park. The pigeons were over the moon.

The building was fumigated and we had to stay out for a whole day. The council started cutting the water off regularly because there was a drought. The canapés from the private view for the exhibition of bread-dough birds went off, and there was an outbreak of diarrhoea. The supermarket delivery boy was replaced; the new one was accused of stealing a tin of jalapeño peppers. The bulb on the third floor went. Someone left the main entrance open and let in the Mormons, who started going from door to door. The salon read *In Search of Lost Time* in a commemorative edition which included all seven volumes of Proust's novel. Four thousand, two hundred and thirty pages long, hardback, with leaves thin as tracing paper and weighing in at almost three and a half kilos (those with arthritis were excused). Signatures were collected to bring back the previous supermarket delivery boy. The bulb on the first floor went. The cockroaches, cool as cucumbers.

My mother had taken less than a week to find a substitute for the dog: an insufferable mutt she had christened Turnup, because it just turned up one day at the front door and started to scratch it. Turnup would eat anything within reach of his muzzle, not just stockings, but my mother imagined it was the reincarnation of that other dog she had loved so much. She didn't say this, of course, but she didn't need to: she would regularly forget herself and call Turnup by the deceased dog's name. Over the ten years he was alive, that dog managed to eat every object in the house that wasn't nailed down, including clothes pegs, refrigerator seals and tons of tubes of toothpaste, which were his weakness: if someone left the bathroom door open, he would jump up and knock over the glass where we kept them. Despite this he never got fat, and remained skeletal until the end of his days. My mother forgave him everything while punishing me and my sister for the slightest offence. We really had it in for that dog. Mum would ground us for a week for any misdemeanour, as this was how she solved everything in life, by locking us up. This meant being condemned to evenings of tedium, spent begging my mother to lift the punishment. In retrospect, the faith placed by that generation in punishment as a way of building character seems astonishing.

Mum worked in the post office in the mornings and in the afternoons she took washing in at home. When we were grounded, we set to following her around, like two little street hawkers, asking: 'What are we supposed to do shut up at home all day? What are we supposed to do shut up at home all day?'

Everything was said in duplicate, like the paperwork for some sort of official procedure, and in a way it was: an official procedure doomed to failure because the bureaucrat on duty, my mother, had an endless supply of patience.

'Go and do your homework,' she ordered us.

We scribbled down our homework and went back to the other work, trying to wear my mother down so she'd let us go and play in the street.

'What are we supposed to do now? What are we supposed to do now?'

'Study.'

'We've studied already,' we lied.

'Go and play.'

'Play what?'

'I don't know, whatever you like.'

We walked around the house, fiddling with things; I started kicking a ball about and it went whizzing past the china cabinet, my sister pulled her doll's head off and said she needed to go to the shop to buy some glue. We returned to the attack.

'What are we supposed to do now? What are we supposed to do now?'

Then my mother would fetch some blank sheets of the paper she used to bring home from the post office, a pack of colouring pencils that had been Dad's and which she kept on top of a wardrobe, and pronounced the final sentence:

'Go and do some drawing.'

Drawing was an activity that never ran out, you could do it for hours and hours, and my mother was very careful to ensure there were always adequate supplies of paper. She grounded us so often that it became a habit, and the day came when Mum had to replace the colouring pencils and then we started drawing even when we weren't being punished. We went out into the streets and began drawing outside, which was something we remembered having seen Dad do.

Punishments came and went, and in the end I asked my mother at least to buy me a sketch pad to give some focus to my endless drawing. I began walking about, up and down, carrying that damn sketchbook, which gave me a reputation for being an artist – and a drifter – in the neighbourhood. For a time it even turned into a lucrative activity: people would pay me to paint portraits of their girlfriends and I would swap the drawings for marbles, initially, and then later on, for my first cigarettes. Then the neighbours grew bored of the artist and my sketchbook lost its cachet, and finally turned into a dreadful burden.

It hadn't rained for almost two months, the Río Lerma was not much more than a stream and the lack of water in our building was making the pipes grumble. In the lobby they were saying that the pipes were *squealing* and, claiming that they couldn't concentrate, the members of the salon decided to go and read in the Jardín de Epicuro. They paid a boy to bring their copies of *In Search of Lost Time* back and forth in a wheelbarrow. From the balcony of my apartment I saw the procession that spanned two blocks of Calle Basilia Franco, each person carrying a foldable Corona chair and turning left at Avenida Teodoro Flores, where they still had three blocks to go, and the little boy sweating and stopping to catch his breath after five steps. I yelled out to them: 'The weight of literature! You're going to kill the poor little squirt!'

The entire salon then had to leave the Jardín de Epicuro because there was a dog that kept hurling itself at them. The mutt was running between the salon members' legs, scratching their ankles with its claws and trying to sharpen its teeth on the covers of the *Lost Times*. The final straw was when the animal tried to mount Francesca, clinging on and rubbing its genitals against her leg: it took the intervention of a passing kid to free her from the canine embrace. In an attempt to keep the salonists away from our block, I suggested they give the dog a stocking. The stocking came back; the dog had refused to eat it. I asked them to show me the hosiery: it was one of Hipólita's, who wore special varicose-vein stockings. I told them to give the dog a normal stocking, made of nylon, and they went off to buy a pair in the haberdashery store. They returned, and the dog still wouldn't go for it. I suggested they stuff one stocking with meat and roll it into a ball, without knotting it, so it would unroll in the mutt's intestines. The butcher gave them a load of skins for free. Problem solved.

With the dog dead, the salon returned to the Jardín de Epicuro to opine, in a break from Proust, that one defect of my novel, which didn't exist, was that I avoided talking about illness in it. Francesca told me so in the lift as we went up to the third floor after returning from our respective activities: I, from drinking the fourth and fifth beer of the day in the greengrocer's shop, she from the salon. We hadn't even reached the first floor and I'd had to put up with a speech on decrepitude as a fundamental theme of the twentieth-century European novel.

'Don't move,' I interrupted her.

And I stamped on two cockroaches, one with my right foot, one with my left.

'You see?' Francesca said. 'You don't listen to me, you're running away from the topic.'

'The cockroaches are running away, I'm not running from anything.'

Between the first and second floors she tried to instruct me on something she referred to as 'the literature of experience' and which basically turned out to mean that one can only write about what one has experienced, about what one knows first-hand. I thought that this was like saying no one can explain what a dog-meat taco tastes like if they haven't eaten one. If they don't believe they've eaten one. If they don't know they've eaten one. The fact is that everyone has eaten a dog-meat taco, even if they don't know it, everyone knows what a dog-meat taco tastes like, even if no one thinks they do. This was the real paradox: not being able to write about something, not because one hadn't experienced it but rather because one didn't know one had experienced it. I'd got distracted, just for a change, and when we got to the third floor I clutched at a loose phrase: 'The experience of illness is as good as any other,' Francesca was saying.

'Is it now! As good as romance, adventure, a journey or freedom?'

'I'm talking about literature.'

'Oh, right! And how would it improve my supposed novel if I started noting down the symptoms of bunions, gastric reflux, hay fever or fatty liver disease? What would the novel be for, inspiring pity? We can do that on our own, we don't need books!'

'Disease is the perfect metaphor for death, decadence, the finite nature of everything human.'

'You mean instead of asking medical questions we should be asking rhetorical questions?'

'You're just like a child. Why do you act the *enfant terrible*? You're running away from reality, just look at the state you're in – do you think I don't know about all your ailments?'

'Since when does reality matter? I feel stronger than a horse.'

Her face flushed with colour, even though the zip had just finished its ascent: the lift doors were opening. As we went our separate ways, I took advantage of the bulb that had blown on the landing to give her bum a squeeze. It was firm yet soft, a most agreeable revelation. The slap echoed around the walls of the corridor until the end of time.

One of the daily battles in the building was keeping the main door closed so we didn't get any old Tom, Dick or Harry coming in. If anyone forgot, Francesca would call an immediate extraordinary general meeting of the Residents' Association, which no one could get out of until the culprit had been found. She took disciplinary measures that ranged from simple tellings-off to fines that wound up in the jar where cash for unexpected building repairs was kept. The woman would have given both Breton and Stalin a run for their money. Following the famous Mormon incident, the discussion got as far as debating the need for a doorman. Everyone referred to it the same way: the day the Mormons got in. It even became a temporal reference point. People would say: a week before the Mormons got in. Or: two days after the Mormons got in. Things happened before or after the day the Mormons got in.

It had happened one Wednesday afternoon, while I was drinking a beer and doggedly pressing a little button on the TV remote after I'd come across the shock of mad-scientist hair and mischievous face of Sergei Eisenstein. That's when someone knocked at the door. They knocked, I mean, at *my* door, not the main door to the building, and that could only mean one thing. Actually, one of many things, which in the end came down to the same thing: Avon ladies, hungry children, drug addicts asking for change, phone company salespeople, talking mutes, seeing blind people, door-to-door kidnappers and shameless scroungers who hadn't even bothered to come up with a story to inspire pity. The only ones who had disappeared, as a symbol of humanity's progress, were the encyclopaedia salesmen. Knowing this perfectly well, I had no plans to open the door, so I ignored the knocking and carried on watching my programme. The knocking didn't stop and I didn't stop ignoring the knocking, either. The ads came on and the pounding on the door continued. Whoever it was was displaying the determination of a zealot.

I opened the door and saw a tall blond young man, transparent as a grub. He was wearing a short-sleeved white shirt, a pair of black trousers and had a little badge at the height of his heart with his name on it, a name that sounded like a Dutch painter of still lifes: *Willem Heda.* Very appropriate: as the hall light wasn't working, he loomed up out of the chiaroscuro. Judging by his appearance I guessed he couldn't be more than twenty, and was carrying out the mission of having doors slammed in his face in a poor country before going to university. In the unlikely event, that was, that going to university wasn't a sin.

'I bring yuh the word of the Lard,' he said.

'Great,' I replied. 'How much per ounce?'

He raised his blond eyebrows in surprise and they almost reached his hair. Then he looked down at the Bible in his right hand. I reached out my left one and rescued the *Aesthetic Theory* from the shelf by the door, where I kept it like a shotgun, just in case. He looked at the tome pulsating in my hand and his eyebrows reached the back of his neck.

'Are yuh a perfessor?'

'As if.'

'I ask becuhse of the book.'

We both looked down at my left hand. He looked at the book as though it were a dog that needed a lead, as though it were a sin to have a book loose in the house.

'This? It's from the library, but don't worry, it doesn't bite.'

'I bring yuh the word of the Lard,' he said again. 'D'yuh have five minutes t'spare?'

I could hear that the ads had finished and my programme was starting again. I held up the *Aesthetic Theory*, opened it at random and began to read: 'To survive reality at its most extreme and grim, artworks that do not want to sell themselves as consolation must equate themselves with that reality.'

He held up his Bible, opened it at random and began to read: 'I have seen all the warks that are done under the sun; and, behold, all is vanity'n vexation of sperit. Ecclesiastes 1:14.'

I started reading again: 'Advanced art writes the comedy of the tragic: Here the sublime and play converge . . . Important artworks nevertheless seek to incorporate this art-alien layer. When, suspected of being infantile, it is absent from art, when the last trace of the vagrant fiddler disappears from the spiritual chamber musician and the illusionless drama has lost the magic of the stage, art has capitulated.'

And he read: 'An' I gave my heart t'know wisdom, and t'know madness and fawlly: I purceived that this also is vexation of sperit. Far in much wisdom is much grief: and he that increaseth knowledge increaseth sarrow.'

I looked from one book to the other: his was bigger. On the TV the programme was still on and I was missing it. I backed up so he could come in.

'Come in, quickly. What'll you have to drink, Villem?'

'It's pernounced "*Will*-em".'

'Thanks for correcting me! A beer, Villem?'

'A glass of wahder. Beer is a sin.'

'No shit! Sit down, there's a really good programme on.'

'What's it about?'

'Scheming and affairs and how to get money for old rope.'

He took off the rucksack he had on his back and sat down on a folding chair, an aluminium one with the Corona beer logo on it. Thief robbing a thief. I sat down on the little armchair I had in front of the TV.

'What's yoah name?' he asked.

'Teo.'

'Mateo?'

'As if.'

'Jus' Teo?'

'Teodoro.'

'Like the awthor of the book?'

'No, the guy who wrote the book's called Theodor.'

'It's the same.'

'It's not the same. He's got an extra "h" and he's missing an "o".'

'Do yuh live alone?'

'Could you let me watch my programme?'

He resigned himself to staring at the screen, where they were showing, one after another, black-and-white photographs taken in the Casa Azul.

'Who's the lady with the moustache?' Willem asked.

'What do you mean? That's Frida Kahlo, the painter. Don't tell me you don't know who she is, even the Indians in the Amazon rainforest know who she is. She's so famous they put up a statue of her in a park in a village of a hundred inhabitants in Uzbekistan, and Bulgaria and Denmark invented their own International Day of Frida Kahlo. See the guy with his trousers pulled up to his armpits? That's Diego Rivera, the man of the house.'

'I'd like to talk t'yuh about the word of the Lard. The word of the Lard is a great comfart for older people.'

I shot him a deadly look.

'Pay attention.'

On the TV they were saying: *she wanted to improvise her own freedom, in order elegantly to overcome a life of pain.*

'They really like suffering, Villem; what does elegance have to do with pain?'

'Pain leads to the Lard.'

'And elegance to hell. By the way, you look pretty elegant, that's a neat little outfit you've got on.'

He flushed: the pigmentation of embarrassment transformed him from a larva into a shrimp, or from a raw shrimp into a cooked shrimp.

'Don't worry,' I said soothingly, 'it was a joke.'

On the screen they were showing images of Frida and Diego, Eisenstein, Dolores del Río, Arcady Boytler, Miguel Covarrubias, María Izquierdo, Xavier Villaurrutia, Adolfo Best Maugard, Lola and Manuel Álvarez Bravo, Trotsky, Juan O'Gorman and Pita Amor. Willem looked at the television and then stopped looking, inspecting my apartment in search of something that would let him start a conversation, and he thought he'd found it when he saw the painting hanging on the opposite wall.

'Is that a clown?' he asked.

'It's a portrait of my mother,' I replied.

'I'm sarry,' he said, flushing again.

'What are you sorry for – for having said my mother is a clown or for not having the sensitivity to appreciate art?'

He thought for a minute, confused.

'Would yuh rather I came back another day?'

'Don't you want to watch the programme?'

'I wanted to talk about the word of the Lard.'

'Come back another day, then. If you're lucky I might even open the door!'

It occurred to him to start coming twice a week, on Wednesdays and Saturdays, and it occurred to me to let him in, just to pass the time. When he found me in a listless mood or when I'd simply run out of beer, he would start preaching at me.

'Yuh still have time to repent.'

'Are you telling me I'm going to die?' I answered.

'It's never too late to repent.'

'What – for having let you in that first day? I wish!'

Following a catechism manual, I suppose, he spent his time repeating that I was his mission, that he had come to Mexico to bring me the word of the Lord. And I replied: 'You got here far too late, Villem, we've already had a load of those types: Franciscans, Dominicans, Humboldt, Rugendas, Artaud, Breton, Burroughs, Kerouac. The competition's tough as hell!'

One day he tried to take a photo of me on his phone to send back to his family, who lived in a small town in Utah.

'You're making a mistake,' I stopped him. 'I'm not a stray dog.'

Dad sent a letter: he'd gone to live by the sea, just like President Ruiz Cortines wanted everyone to do. He was living in
Manzanillo, with a job processing paperwork in the port.
The letter was to my sister and me, and was written in blue
ink in tiny, cramped handwriting, the letters all leaning to
the right as if they were falling asleep. It was just one page
but it took us a whole afternoon to decipher it. He said that
ships arrived in the port from the United States and from
China and that last week there had been a north wind and
he'd seen thirty-foot-high waves. We had never seen the sea,
although we guessed this was meant to impress us. He said
that the president of Manzanillo used to be a painter and a
taxi driver, and that this proved how far anyone could go in
life simply by making up their minds and persevering. He
also told us he'd started painting again, and that he would
get together after work with a group of artists on the docks
to paint seascapes, and had sold an impressionist painting of
a fishing boat to a tourist from Guadalajara. Then came the
last part, the reason for the letter and the bit that took us the
longest to understand, because in addition to the handwriting,
we weren't old enough yet to comprehend other-worldly
aspirations. My father was requesting that when he died, we

incinerate him and scatter his ashes in an art gallery, 'where they belonged'. He said he wanted the dust from his bones to float among the artworks and be breathed in by sensitive people, 'sticking to their clothes and travelling around on the threadbare lapels of new artists' coats'. Along with the note, my father had sent us three pesos: the cost of four and a half pounds of beans. Mum refused to read it, but when we went to bed we left it on the kitchen table, as if we'd forgotten it. I discovered later that the president of Manzanillo had been a house painter, not a painter of pictures, as I'd thought for some time. And that he'd been the leader of the taxi drivers' union, which contradicted my father's motivational theories. Thesis. Antithesis. So life went on.

I went to look for the dog's body in the Jardín de Epicuro and found it under some bushes, where it had dragged itself to try and puke up the stocking. I couldn't believe it: it was a Labrador, huge and black. Or rather, yes, I could believe it: I knew I was dealing with literary fundamentalists, people capable of killing a family pet and, on top of that, of abandoning the body for no good reason other than to preserve the sacrosanct peace they needed to concentrate on their reading and dilettantism. I covered the corpse with a pile of twigs and leaves and walked over to the butcher's on the corner, the same one that had given the salon members the deadly animal skins.

I didn't know the butcher, having never needed to avail myself of his services until that day. From Monday to Saturday I ate in a budget restaurant and on Sundays I made do with bar snacks from the place on the corner. I sat down to wait on the bench outside the shop until there were no customers around to mess up the operation. I had to wait fifteen, twenty minutes. Eventually I was able to go in and I wasted no time; I couldn't risk someone coming in and surprising us halfway through the negotiation.

'I'll sell you a dog,' I announced.

'What?' replied the butcher.

He was carving a piece of meat that didn't look like beef, or pork, or anything advertised on the colourful posters pinned to the walls.

'I'll sell you a dog,' I said again.

He let his knife fall, looked up and quivered behind his apron covered in blood as if his ribcage were a barrel full of tacks in an earthquake.

'What the hell are you talking about?'

'I've got a dog just around the corner, in the Jardín de Epicuro. It's just died, it's perfectly healthy, it choked on a stocking.'

'A dog?'

'It's a Labrador, it must weigh between thirty and forty kilos. The whole thing's yours to use if you want it.'

The butcher picked up his knife again, but did not resume his task. I feared the implement would interpret the signals the butcher was sending it and decide to switch roles: from work tool to murder weapon.

'Is this a joke?' he said.

'Don't play dumb, I was a taco seller my whole life, I had a stand in the Candelaria de los Patos. I know perfectly well how this works.'

'Are you a health inspector?'

'At my age? If they raised the retirement age that much even the dead would have to start working.'

'Empty your pockets, show me your wallet.'

I obeyed, striving to show him I didn't represent any organisation or institution concerned with the illegal trade in dog meat or the observation of hygiene standards in butchers' shops. This was easy, because as well as not representing these organisations, I didn't look like I did either.

'You see?' I said. 'You can trust me.'

'I'll give you some advice: go and see your geriatric specialist and tell him you're losing touch with reality.'

'Are you going to keep acting dumb? What's that meat you're cutting? I'll tell you one thing, it's not beef or pork. Who are you trying to kid?'

'This?' he said, pointing at the chunks of meat with the tip of his knife. 'This is horse, Grandpa.'

'If you don't want to buy it I'll pay you to chop it up for me. How much would you charge? I'm sure I can flog it to a taco seller.'

He raised his knife and pointed straight ahead with it, not threateningly, just using it to indicate the shop door. One of the indisputable advantages of being old is that most people end up taking pity on little old men, even if they don't deserve it. It's enough to make you become a serial killer.

'You're even more cracked than you look,' he said. 'If you don't beat it now I'm going to call the police.'

I walked out and mentally ran through my daily stroll to see if I could recall another butcher. Nothing. I sat down to think on a bench in the Jardín de Epicuro; it seemed to me some sort of conclusion had to be drawn from what had just happened. How was it possible that a specimen weighing at least thirty kilos, strong, healthy and well-fed, could end up on the rubbish heap or, even worse, buried? All of a sudden I felt infinitely old, as old as the world. The country had changed, it wasn't the same any more, it was a place I no longer recognised: this was why the tacos were so bad.

I was about to get up from the bench to plod slowly back home when I heard the shout: 'Here he is, ma'am!'

A maid in uniform was crouching near the bush where the dog's corpse lay. Behind me, a 4 x 4 pulled up with a squeal of tyres, one of those cars made by gringos for one of their endless wars. There were potholes the size of trenches in the road, but even so this was over the top: Iraq was a long way off. A young couple got out and ran towards the park, with three children following them. The maid shouted again: 'No! Not the children!'

The mother, or the woman I guessed was the mother, turned and encircled them in an embrace to stop them coming any further. The man came over to the dog's corpse.

'Fuck,' he said.

And then he shouted:

'Take the kids, take them away!'

I suddenly became sixty years younger. I stood up and, with an energetic, almost military gait, marched over to the greengrocer's. I could almost hear the strains of the 'Ode to Joy' in my head and I easily broke the world record for urban hiking for the over-sixties.

I found Juliet spraying tomatoes with water and covering them with plastic so as to speed up and complete the rotting process. I called out from the door:

'I've got news! A great victory for the Revolution!'

'Calm down, Bakunin. Want a beer?'

'A tequila'd be more appropriate.'

Three tequilas later and, thanks to the story of my feat, I was about to convince her to come up to my apartment. I failed at the last moment: 'I'll nip to the chemist and pick you up on the way back.'

I stared hard at her mouth, at her full upper lip which, when she smiled, formed a little pout beneath her nose: a second smile.

'Why are you looking at me like that?' she asked.

'Why do you think?' I replied.

She pursed her lips and the double smile disappeared.

'Let's leave it there,' Juliet said, with all the gentleness sincere rejections tend to have. 'You and I have more important deeds awaiting us. Let's not jeopardise the Revolution for a shag.'

'Isn't it the other way round, *Juliette*?'

'What do you mean, the other way round?'

'That it's not worth jeopardising a shag for the Revolution?'

'You're such a clown.'

I went back home and had to make do with the company of Willem, who was waiting for me in the lobby, sitting on the floor in front of the lift doors, behind the circle of the salon.

'What are you doing here? Who let you in?'

'They did.'

We got into the lift and I waited for the doors to close and the contraption to start moving before asking: 'What did they say to you?'

'They assed me lats of questions.'

'Who, Francesca?'

'Yeah, she talked to me in English.'

'What did she want to know?'

'Why I come to see yuh.'

'What did you tell her?'

'I said I come to talk. To talk about the word of the Lard. And sometimes we watch TV.'

'Good. Hey, how does she speak?'

'What?'

'How well does she speak English?'

'She speaks as if she wus teaching a child.'

'Just like in Spanish!'

'Why are they so innersted in me coming?'
'They probably think you're a poof.'
His eyebrows reached his shoulder blades.
'They read a lot of novels,' I explained.

Everyone attended the meeting, as was customary: meetings took place in the lobby and all the residents, except me, spent their lives down there. Depending on the topic, sometimes I showed up and sometimes I didn't. I went just enough so as not to fall foul of an administrative rule that meant Francesca would report me to the management committee. On this occasion I had decided to go because the matter affected me directly: the local supermarket had replaced our delivery boy, who had been helping us carry our shopping for over a year, and the entire building considered it an outrage. They said that the new boy refused to do anything other than leave the shopping bags at the entrance to the apartments. The previous one had always been happy to change a light bulb, kill a particularly insidious cockroach, move a piece of furniture, stand on a chair and get something down from the top of a wardrobe . . .

The new boy was cocky and, instead of helping, he delivered speeches from the Mexico City Union of Deliverymen and alleged that what we asked him to do was not included in the job description drawn up by the union. He kept a folded copy in his trouser pocket, and was always quoting huffily at us from it. Then he would take offence because he didn't get a tip, or the tip wasn't big enough. As if that wasn't enough, the previous delivery boy had been a first-rate spiv. I'd bought a microwave oven off him, a DVD recorder, a little radio with headphones and a cordless phone. And most importantly: he used to supply me with a whisky distilled in Tlalnepantla that cost thirty pesos a litre. When I asked the new boy if he could get it for me, he replied indignantly that he was from Iztapalapa.

In response to the residents' furious complaints comparing the new delivery boy to the old, the manager of the supermarket had said that we would soon become accustomed to the change, as if the prevailing economic model had transformed capacity for adaptation into a corporate form of resignation. Then someone on the ground floor accused the new delivery boy of stealing a tin of jalapeños, and the cup of patience spilled over.

The committee drew up a petition to sign, *demanding* the new delivery boy be dismissed and the old one be immediately reinstated. The discussion about whether the letter should 'demand' or 'request' took two whole afternoons which I, if I'm honest, spent going back and forth between the lobby and the bar, between the bar and the greengrocer's, and the greengrocer's and the lobby, and around again. Juliet said:

'Typical intellectuals, trying to put the world to rights with letters. If they just kidnapped one of the cashiers, the supermarket would give the old delivery boy his job back within twenty minutes!'

The manager of the supermarket replied, the moment he was handed the letter, that no matter how much he wanted to he was unable to meet our demands because the previous delivery boy had simply stopped showing up for work one day. To demonstrate his goodwill, he gave us the boy's address and promised us that if we could persuade him to return, as long as he could provide some kind of documentation justifying his absence, then he, the manager, would give the kid his job back.

An expedition was organised to visit him: Francesca, in her role as president of the committee, and me, in my role as customer with an urgent need to ensure a supply of provisions. We crossed the city by metro, taxi, local train, bus, another taxi. A journey of three and a half hours, during which Francesca gave me a lesson in Aristotelian *hypokrisis*, for having committed the error of asking her where she'd learned to hold forth the way she did. She then classified fifty Mexican novels, dividing them into urban and rural, expounded upon what she called 'the fallacies of structuralism', which put me in a dark mood as I recalled buildings collapsing in earthquakes, and finished by explaining (by which point I had, for a change, lost concentration) an approach to narration known as 'free indirect style', at which point I no longer knew if we were talking about literature or swimming. Until at last we arrived at the door of an apartment in a complex in Tlalnepantla, which I began desperately pounding on.

The door was opened by the boy's mother, drying her hands on a checked apron, even though they appeared to be dry. The apartment looked a lot like the one we each had back home, including the cockroaches: a bedroom, a kitchenette, a bathroom and a room that served as living and dining room. Except that four people were living here, not one. Three now: the delivery boy's father, mother and younger brother. Three now – because the delivery boy had disappeared. His mother told us what she knew, that he had simply not come home from work one day. From the kitchen, a cockroach peeped out, waving its antennae: I could have sworn I'd seen it in my apartment. We asked her if she'd reported the disappearance, what she'd said to the police. The mother turned to look at a calendar on the wall, from 2009, with photos of dogs and the red logo of a dog-food manufacturer where my sister had worked over fifty years ago. She dried her hands on her apron again, even though they were dry, looked at the dog on the calendar and said: 'They told us he was mixed up in drugs, that he was selling drugs.'

She started to cry as if her son had been accused of stabbing a thousand puppies to death. Francesca tried to console her: she told her that the police always said that when someone disappeared, so they didn't have to look for them. That the delivery boy was a good kid and the proof was that we had come looking for him. That everyone in our building missed him, we'd grown very fond of him. It sounded as if she was talking about a dog. She paused so I could back her up.

'Very fond,' I said.

'How old was your son?' Francesca asked.

And immediately corrected herself, making things worse: 'How old *is* he, I mean?'

'Seventeen,' his mother replied.

'He looked older,' Francesca said.

'Yes, he *looks* older,' I said.

'Life's not easy round here,' said his mother.

She was apologising because her son had had to grow up quicker than she would have liked, hinting, as she did so, that she believed the police's version of events and ultimately justifying the boy's actions as inevitable. The boy's younger brother came out of the bedroom where he'd been, behind the closed door, until now. His mother introduced him, said he was fifteen, was at college, a smart kid who would probably go to university. At that moment I saw my chance and I wasn't going to let it go: I asked the boy's mother if I could speak to him alone. I winked, hoping the mother and Francesca would realise what my intentions were. The false ones, not the actual ones.

'Yes, of course,' the mother said.

I stood up and walked over to the door. The boy followed me, obediently. We left the apartment and moved a few yards away down the hallway.

'Are you selling?' I asked him.

'How much?' he said.

'Three litres.'

'Litres? How many grams, Grandpa?'

'I want to buy whisky, kid, and don't call me Grandpa. Can you get hold of it?'

'Hang on,' he replied.

He walked to the end of the hall and knocked on the last door. I watched him wait outside. Then he returned, carrying a bag. I gave him a hundred-peso note and he gave me the three bottles.

'You're twenty pesos short,' he said.

'Your brother used to sell it to me for thirty.'

'I charge forty.'

I gave him the twenty pesos.

'Do you know what happened to your brother?' I asked.

'They say he got whacked.'

'Who says?'

'People here, in the building.'

I put the bottles in the rucksack I'd brought along for the purpose.

'Hey, don't tell my mother,' the boy said.

Don't tell her what, I thought: that you know your brother's dead or that you're headed the same way?

'Could you deliver to my apartment?' I asked him.

'Not likely, I'm not going all that way just to earn ten pesos. My brother was a pushover.'

The manager of the supermarket fired the new delivery boy after accusing him of having stolen the tin of jalapeños and a new new delivery boy was hired. After he got wise to what had happened to his predecessor, the new new delivery boy gave us a wide berth, and when we did get hold of him, we had to beg him to come in with us on the plan. In the end he set a condition: seizing upon some small print in the union's collective agreement that the other boy hadn't read, he refused to cross the threshold of the building.

Willem had decided to exterminate the cockroaches. One day he had brought along a piece of chalk and traced around the outline of the apartment and all the rooms, as if he were drawing a blueprint on top of reality. The theory was that the cockroaches wouldn't be able to cross the line and would remain outside.

'And the ones that are already inside won't be able to leave?' I asked him.

He promised he'd bring another solution for the ones inside. Logically, the cockroaches crossed the line as if nothing had changed: since when did borders work? Another day Willem had gone round the whole house with a spray gun. That day, while the poison took effect, we had gone to have a coffee in the Chinese restaurant over the road. Actually, my coffee was a beer. They gave us fortune cookies. Willem's said: *You will be recompensed for your good deeds.* Mine said: *He who seeks, finds.*

'I knew it!' Willem said.

All that Bible study just to end up interpreting everything literally. Then it dawned on me that there weren't any cockroaches in the Chinese restaurant. We tried to talk to the owner, the guy who looked like the owner, and to the waiters. Impossible: they only spoke Chinese. I tried to take one of them over to my building to show him a cockroach, to see if I could get him to understand that way, but when I tugged at his arm they all took fright and locked themselves in the kitchen. Willem said: 'Perhaps if yuh didn't drink so much.'

'If I didn't drink so much I'd understand Chinese? Yeah, right!'

'If yuh didn't drink so much yuh wouldn' have scayud them.'

'Don't you preach at me, Villem.'

When we got back to the apartment, the cockroaches were merrily strolling about on the ceiling. Another time, Willem had installed traps in every corner of the place, these little black plastic boxes. I never understood how they worked: were the cockroaches going to lift up the little boxes and get inside? That idea didn't work either, but at least it was intriguing. It kept my brain occupied for a whole week. Just as mysterious were the plug-ins, which in theory gave off a substance that would flush out the critters. Equally ineffective. A yellow powder you had to smear on the filler between the tiles on the floor turned out to be the worst of the fiascos: the cockroaches ate it and started flying madly around like rockets. I suggested to Willem that we try it ourselves.

Failures came and went, until finally, one Wednesday afternoon, Willem turned up with his head bowed.

'I've run out of ideas, Teodooruh,' he said.

I had one: we set to smashing them with books.

He, with his Bible, and I with my *Aesthetic Theory*.

The woman next door had got a job and her hours prevented her from collecting her daughter after school, so she had asked if my mother could help get her home safe and sound. The woman was a widow and the little girl her only daughter, and she took classes in the afternoon. I had all my classes in the morning. The girl was fourteen, nearly fifteen.

'Can she not she walk home on her own?' my mother asked.

'You have no idea what an ordeal that would be,' explained our neighbour.

I did: queues would form down the street to follow her long-legged walk home. The street was full of dangers, you only had to open your eyes to the canine show going on to imagine what might end up happening to her. Lines of dogs waiting patiently to mount a little bitch in heat. Or not so patiently: sometimes there were furious fights in the queue. Growls. Fangs. Bloodied hackles. Unwanted pregnancies.

My mother replied that she could count on us, or rather, on me, and told me I could take Turnup out for a walk at the same time. Our neighbour was satisfied: she didn't know that until now I had been one of her daughter's most ardent stalkers.

The girl was called Hilaria, despite evidence to the contrary.

'Why did they call you Hilaria?' I asked her.

'Why do you think?' she replied. 'Listen to my laugh, it's hilarious.'

And she growled.

Every afternoon I waited for her on a bench outside school; Hilaria would cross the road and, before doing anything else, she would walk over to the mirror in a nearby shop window, where she would apply make-up, let down her hair and hitch her skirt up to her knees. Things only got worse: if she already caused an uproar when she walked along dressed like a nun with her mother, now it was like the procession of the Feast of Our Lady of Guadalupe in December. It was a walk of nine blocks and it took us twenty minutes going at the slow pace Turnup obliged us to walk at, pissing here and there, grubbing about in the rubbish in the gutter, seeing what he could stick his snout into. My mother had got it into her head that if we tired the dog out he'd do less damage. When her hypothesis failed, she said that tiring the dog out made him hysterical. What was certain was that, if he was out in the street for a long time, the damage would at least be caused to other people's property.

Sometimes it took us longer, if we had to stop on the way, if we crossed paths with a bitch on heat. Then there was nothing for it: the first few times we'd tried to walk on by and Turnup had snapped at our ankles. Knowing full well how uncooperative he was, we had to wait our turn with the other dogs. I looked beyond Hilaria, at the other queue, the queue of guys ogling her. Until at last, it was our dog's turn. Turnup was medium-sized, a big dog by the street's standards. He mounted bitches easily, skilfully. Hilaria watched the spectacle and asked me: 'Does it turn you on, Teo?'

I tried to put my hand over my crotch so she couldn't see what was going on underneath it, and she thumped me on the back with a petulant smile and said: 'Pervert.'

The days came and went, and I took advantage of the routine to carry out my own pursuit, armed with my sketchbook.

'Will you let me draw you?'

'How do you mean?'

'I want to make a portrait of you, I'm an artist.'

'I know that, everyone knows that, they say your mum ended up with a right dud with you, that you're a fat lot of good to her. I meant how do you want to draw me, how would you do it?'

'A nice portrait, nothing avant-garde.'

'Nude?'

Beneath my fly I suddenly felt my erection, rising up and up, leaving me without an answer.

'Does it turn you on, Teo?'

I swallowed hard and started to imagine her long naked legs and everything else, which, truth be told, I didn't even know how to imagine, so inexperienced was I.

'Tomorrow,' she promised, 'before my mum gets home.'

'A portrait takes several days.'

'I knew it! You're a sleazebag.'

The following day, I told her:

'I've got a new sketchbook.'

'And how are you going to draw me?'

I was slowly growing less timid, emboldened by her provocations, and getting used to discussing these things with a great deal of blood in my groin and very little in my head.

'First I've got to look at you for a long time to concentrate, I have to find a style, it's not just about copying your figure.'

'Look at me for ages, eh? With my legs open?'

'Maybe,' I replied, my trousers wet.

'I knew it! You're sick. I can't do it today, my mother's coming home early. Tomorrow.'

The hours came and went, long as years, and eventually the next day arrived.

'Have you got any ice?'

'Ice? What for?'

'No ice, no portrait.'

'Why?'

'What do you mean, why? I need ice to put on my nipples so they stand up nice and stiff.'

Under my fly, my erection howled.

'Get some ice. Tomorrow.'

Tomorrow, of course, never came; what did come was the day one of her pursuers emerged from anonymity. He wasn't one of the usual ones, although he did seem vaguely familiar and I was sure I'd seen him before. We were at Hilaria's front door when he called at us to wait for him. He was an older guy, fat, who wore his trousers pulled up to his chest. Literally: it looked like he needed to clamp his arms close to his body to keep the trousers in place. He took a while to reach us, panting, and he had a spot of paint on his left shoe. He bent down with great difficulty to pat Turnup, who seized his chance to steal and then eat a paintbrush out of the man's overcoat pocket. When the man stood up, even though the dog's lead led to my hand, he acted as if I didn't exist.

'What's your name?' he asked Hilaria.

'Marilín,' she replied, putting the accent on the last syllable.

He asked if she lived there, pointing over to the entrance to our building with his chin. She said she did.

'I'd like to speak to your mother,' the man said.

She said that her mother was working and would get home later.

'How long will she be?' he asked.

'About an hour,' she replied.

The man looked around until he spotted a cheap little restaurant across the road. He said he'd go and have a coffee there, pointing with his chin again at the place, and that when her mother got home to tell her to go and find him there and not to forget. Then he added:

'Tell your mother Diego Rivera wants a word with her.'

The people from the Society for the Protection of Animals came to the building and started going from door to door, downstairs then upstairs, left to right, until they got to mine, the last but one. Interrogations came and went, and by now I was the mastermind of a crime. There were two inspectors: a short young woman with hair down to her waist and a full bust, and her boss, who had a head shaped like a papaya. I didn't make that up, Hipólita pointed it out a little later; she was from Veracruz and familiar with the fruit. She even specified that it looked like a Maradol papaya and Juliet, who was the nearest thing we had to a botanist, corroborated this: you simply had to place the fruit upright with the part that had been connected to the stalk pointing downwards, for the chin.

I tried to defend myself, arguing that the dog's death was related to the literary salon which I was not a member of – besides, I didn't even read novels.

'Don't lie,' Papaya-Head said. 'I know you're writing one as we speak.'

'I am not writing a novel, who told you that?'

'Everyone, from 1-A to 3-B. That's how they refer to you, didn't you know? They call you "the one who's writing a novel".'

I was going to reflect that Francesca's obsession had now turned into collective psychosis, but there was no time: Papaya-Head was set on reprimanding me. He claimed he had talked to the local butcher and that my appearance matched the description of an old man who had tried to sell him a dog. The same appearance, to make matters worse, as that described by the man who had filed the complaint, who purported to have seen an old man whistling the 'Ode to Joy' in a euphoric manner in the Jardín de Epicuro while he and his family wept over the death of their dog. He took a sheet of paper from a bulging file and announced: 'Here is the report.'

Then he read out: 'Dark-skinned man over eighty years of age, mestizo, messy white hair, average height, tubercular nose, light brown eyes, rat-like ears, contemptuous, cynical expression, no identifying marks or scars.'

He paused and uttered the last word emphatically, as if in the document it were underlined in red ink: '*Drunk.*'

'I'm seventy-eight!' I protested.

'That doesn't matter,' replied Papaya-Head. 'People are terrible at calculating ages. And, no offence, but you do look pretty decrepit.'

'And what's all that about a "tubercular nose"?' I asked.

'Like a potato,' Papaya-Head said.

'It looks more like a turnip,' the young woman said.

'Tubercular comes from tuberculosis,' I said, trying to correct them.

'Well in this case it comes from tuber,' Papaya-Head said.

'Well that's not right, how can you trust the description of someone who doesn't even know how to use adjectives? And anyway, a turnip is not a tuber.'

Papaya-Head turned to look at the young woman indul-
gently, excusing her mistake. It was clear he saw himself
as her mentor, the one responsible for teaching her how to
pester people.

'Writers, eh?' he said to her.

'I'm not a writer!' I complained.

'So tell us what these notebooks are, then.'

He pointed an accusing finger towards the shelf by the
front door and continued: 'If, as you say, you're not writing
a novel, you won't mind if we analyse the contents of your
notebooks, will you?'

'Do you have a search warrant?' I replied.

'I knew it!' he cried, clapping his hands together gleefully
at the same time.

'Do you mind telling me what I'm being accused of? Being
a writer? I declare myself innocent!'

Then he said he had a statement that incriminated me:
Hipólita had cracked. He took another sheet of paper from
his file and held it up next to his papaya head: 'Hipólita, the
lady from 2-C, has stated, and I quote: "The man who's writing a novel recommended we give the dog a stocking to eat."
End of quote. The murder method matches the results of the
autopsy carried out on the animal.'

'It's not me! How many times do I have to tell you I'm not
writing a novel?'

'Hipólita, the lady from 2-C, has stated, and again I quote:
"The man who's writing a novel lives in 3-C." End of quote.'

I assumed it was revenge for not putting her in my supposed
novel, or for writing about her moustache. Then I found out
it was neither one nor the other: Hipólita had fractured her
right wrist while turning over a page of the Proust and was on

some painkillers that had loosened her tongue (and gave her hallucinations, like seeing papayas where there were heads).

'Are you aware of Mexico City's law against cruelty to animals?' Papaya-Head said, threateningly.

I didn't reply either way; I assumed there was a law for the elderly that would save me from all this. If the city's governors liked anything it was these very two things: animals and old people. I imagined that the second group still took precedence. At that moment, the doorbell went: it was Wednesday; it was Willem. I spoke into the intercom and told him to come on up, then announced: 'I'd like to call a witness.'

'This isn't a trial,' Papaya-Head said.

'The witness will refute your accusation,' I replied.

We waited. Willem took ages, just for a change. A cockroach emerged from the kitchen; its antennae detected the tension of the moment and it quickly went back in. The young woman walked over to the painting hanging on the wall and stood looking at it for a long time, then said: 'Did you paint this, sir?'

'No, my father did.'

'Is it your mother? Your father's wife, I mean.'

'Yes.'

'She must have been very pretty.'

I looked at her closely, up and down and then down and up.

'What did you say you were called?' I asked her.

'Dorotea.'

The minute Papaya-Head was getting ready to upbraid the girl for her soft-hearted tactfulness, someone knocked at the door. I opened it. Willem crossed the threshold and Papaya-Head looked at me scornfully: 'Is this a joke?'

He was wearing his knackered old Mormon uniform, his black rucksack on his back, and in his right hand he held the ever-present Bible. Dorotea came over to read the little badge pinned to his shirt: she was so short, and Willem so tall, that her eyes only came up to the level of the boy's heart.

'Pleased to meet you, Willem,' she said.

'Are you Dutch?' Papaya-Head asked.

'I'm from Utah,' Willem replied.

'A gringo,' Papaya-Head concluded.

'Actually, my famly . . . '

'Now's not the time for genealogies, Villem,' I interjected.

I asked him to confirm that the day of the dog's death he had been with me and that I hadn't given any orders, or suggestions, to carry it out.

'What day was it?' he asked.

The young woman told him the date: the day and the month.

'No, sorry. I mean which day of the week was it?' he said.

The report didn't say. We went to look at the calendar I had in the kitchen. The cockroach was amusing itself with a little granule of sugar. The calendar was from 2012, so we had to add a day. We looked: Monday – that is, it had happened on a Tuesday.

'No,' Willem said, 'I only come on Waynesdays.'

'Are you sure?' I asked. 'Are you really sure?'

'And Saturdays,' he concluded.

Papaya-Head left the kitchen and headed for the front door, with a self-important air, as if this were a trial after all.

'Wait!' I shouted. 'Wasn't 2012 a leap year?'

We went back to the calendar: February had twenty-nine days.

This didn't change the calculation in any way, but it did at least sow confusion. The girl took out her phone and was about to look up the date on it. I touched her arm with a shaky hand (I'm really good at that). She took pity on me and put the device away. Papaya-Head held out a copy of the report and a summons, two weeks away. He left, dragging Dorotea's dismay along with him, the girl looking at me as if cruelty to animals were punishable with stoning, chemical castration and hanging, one after the other.

'What the hell is wrong with you, Villem?' I shouted as soon as the door had closed.

'Lahying is aginst Gawd's commandments,' he said.

'God doesn't exist, kiddo, you haven't got a clue.'

I went over to the bookshelf and took down the *Aesthetic Theory*. I was on the verge of throwing it at his head, but what good would that do me? What I should have done was to ask to borrow a copy of *In Search of Lost Time*. The pasty little bastard would never have got out of that one alive.

'I don't want to see you again,' I said, opening the door for him.

He picked up his rucksack and began his pilgrimage towards the exit.

'Hey, before you go, tell me something.'

'What?'

'What's my nose like?'

'What?'

'You heard, what does it look like?'

He stood and looked at my nose, not daring to open his mouth.

'Tell me.'

'A potato?'

'Get out of here, go on, beat it!' I ordered.

He went without a fight: we both knew he'd be back on Saturday. I poured myself a beer and, when I'd calmed down, began to read the police report. And then I noticed the surname of the person who'd filed it. I shot off down the stairs like a ramshackle rocket to the greengrocer's, knocking over the salon's chairs as I went, shouting out as I got there:

'You'll never guess who wants to put me in the slammer!'

Juliet interrupted what she was doing, which was talking to Dorotea.

'Come in, Teo,' said Juliet. 'Let me introduce you to my granddaughter. This is Dorotea.'

'I've already met her,' I replied, 'she works for the dog police. How did you end up with a counter-revolutionary granddaughter?'

'There's nothing counter-revolutionary about it, just the opposite,' said Dorotea, defensively.

'Yeah right! Are dogs going to start the Revolution?'

'Hey, don't laugh,' said Juliet, 'the mutts already run the street. Calm down Teo, Dorotea's a good girl. She's too idealistic, but there you go; she's not her grandmother's granddaughter for nothing.'

'I should go, *Abuela*,' said Dorotea. 'I'll come back another day.'

'But you never come to see me!'

'From now on I will, you'll see.'

She gave Juliet such a tender hug even I forgave her for coming after me.

'And another thing, child,' said Juliet, 'stop sending your friends to my shop, they all owe me money.'

'Collaborate with the cause, *Abue*!'

'I don't have enough tomatoes for so many causes. I have to charge people, otherwise how can I eat?'

They finished their hug and, before she left, Dorotea asked me: 'Is that boy a friend of yours?'

'The Mormon?'

'Uh-huh.'

'Do you like him? Want me to set you up on a date?'

Her long hair stood on end.

'No, no, I was just curious, missionaries have always intrigued me. And besides, I was surprised at his integrity.'

'Integrity?'

'He wasn't prepared to lie to give you an alibi.'

'Well you know what, now that I think about it you two would make a great couple, the traitor and the counter-revolutionary. I *am* going to set you up.'

'I have a boyfriend.'

'A boyfriend?' Juliet interrupted. 'Is this what we fought the Sexual Revolution for?'

'I really am going now, *Abue*,' said Dorotea.

'Hey,' I told her, 'be nice to the kid. He's ten years younger than he looks. Mentally, I mean.'

She left the greengrocer's and Juliet went into the back room, returning with two glasses of beer.

'You're still seeing the Mormon?' she asked. 'He'll end up converting you before long.'

'Don't worry, I've been vaccinated.'

'So?'

'I'm the one who's converting him. The kid lacks experience.'

'Do you feel sorry for him?'

'It's not as if he's a puppy.'

We sipped our beer and, since it wasn't very cold, the foam traced a fleeting moustache onto Juliet's lip.

'I didn't know you had a granddaughter,' I said.

'You never asked me. We waste all our time clowning around. Have you got grandchildren?'

'No.'

'Children?'

'Nope.'

'Didn't you tell me you were a widower?'

'Uh-huh.'

'So you were lying!'

'What does that matter? The family is a bourgeois institution!'

'Maybe you're a poof?'

'Yeah, right.'

'There wouldn't be anything wrong with that. In this greengrocer's we respect all denominations, even Buggeration. Are you sleeping with the little Mormon?'

'Don't push it, *Juliette.*'

'Well then?'

'Well then what?'

'Are you a fake widower?'

'Hey, I didn't come here to talk about this. You want me tell you what happened or not? You have no idea who's going around accusing me!'

Another poet died and the entire literary salon crossed the city to go and bid farewell to him at a funeral parlour (this poet had failed to gain access to the Palacio de Bellas Artes). Everyone had gone except Hipólita, whom I found sitting in the lobby caressing with her left hand a worn-out copy of the poet's poems that was lying in her lap. She had a cast on her right hand.

'Now today I would have liked to trake the mip,' she sighed. 'He was from my tome hown.'

As well as loosening her tongue, the painkillers got it in a twist, switching her letters around.

'From Veracruz?'

'Hm-mmm, from Córboda, like me.'

Hipólita had three children who still lived in Veracruz, from where she had escaped after her husband died and bastards sprouted like mushrooms over his corpse. I went over and looked at the cover of the book, so slim it wouldn't even have served to squash fleas: a drawing of three furious dogs, two of them fighting, rolling around on the ground, and the third, barking at a figurative horizon, which would be located on the spine of the book. Hipólita was stroking them as if trying to calm them down, as if this was what would ensure the poet's soul rested in peace.

'Did you cancel your bread-dough-modelling classes?' I asked.

'Wo, nhy do you ask?'

'Your hand,' I said.

'Oh, that. I've ween borking like this, with one hand. Would you sike to lee?'

She didn't wait for a reply and went into the room we used as a dumping ground. She came back out with a washing-powder box, from which she started removing the little figures with dire dexterity. They were brightly coloured deformed little lumps, violently aborted birds, expelled from the egg and fried in a pan before they could let out a peep. I could tell they were birds because Hipólita and her students had one-track minds; otherwise it would have been possible to imagine they were anything or nothing at all.

'They don't have bittle leaks yet,' she said apologetically. 'I'm going to make those when my hinjury has eeled.'

I peered at a sticky blue mess by the light in the lobby.

'That's a fittle linch,' she explained. 'There's a lot of them in Veracruz.'

The art of modelling with bread dough, which throughout history had been fervently naive and figurative, had just entered, rather abruptly, its abstract period. Hipólita had skipped all previous stages, and thus her contribution would in all likelihood go unacknowledged. Not even art, which is considered a realm of liberty, is open to anomalies: bread-dough modelling would need first to go through impressionism and cubism, at the very least, in order to be able to understand Hipólita's figures as evolution.

'What's that red stuff?' I asked, because I'd noticed all the figures were covered in red blotches.

'That?' she said, pointing at the belly of the supposed finch.

'Uh-huh.'

'It's blood.'

'Are they dead?' I asked.

'Cow han they be dead if they're made of dread bough?' said Hipólita. 'Do you thike lem?'

She began placing the figures carefully back into the detergent box, as I searched for the appropriate words for the situation.

'I think you should keep taking those painkillers you're on.'

I'd signed up in secret for painting classes at La Esmeralda. My sister, who had always been more practical than me and ate papayas instead of looking at them, had gone off to study business. I am able to recognise this only now, almost sixty years later: now my mother was the one who would be punished, in quite a cruel manner. Everything pointed to my sister becoming a secretary. This, along with the length of her legs, horrified my mother. I, meanwhile, was about to repeat the same mistake as my father, who had driven her so mad: confusing passion with vocation. As if it was a matter of genetics, a physical defect or an incurable disease, I was convinced I'd inherited his artistic temperament.

I had gone along to La Esmeralda and discovered very quickly that what really interested me was happening beyond its walls, in the bohemian lives of the students. We used to meet nearby and when the contingent was complete, we'd head for the dingy old bars in the centre. I was enjoying life, I'd found my vocation, until early one morning Turnup stuck his nose into the pocket of the trousers I'd thrown onto the floor by the bed. The next day the dog wouldn't wake up; his breathing was almost imperceptible and he didn't respond, no matter how much my mother shook him. In the afternoon she took him to the vet, who diagnosed him with marijuana poisoning. It was a simple diagnosis, you had only to smell his nose, and if my mother hadn't discovered this earlier it was because she'd never smelled weed. That night, when I got back from 'taking classes' at La Esmeralda, Mum was waiting up for me, sitting in the living room, to tell me what the vet had said. It was a clear accusation, but since I had arrived home in a good mood, a little tipsy, and was in no way about to admit my guilt, I tried to play down the drama.

'Impressive,' I said. 'How did the dog manage to light the spliff?'

Mum said only one thing:

'You do dishearten me.'

I suppose she could have said that I was breaking her heart, but that would have implied a weakness of the muscle in her chest, as if she had a defect that meant she couldn't deal with disappointments and the disheartening was partly her fault. Instead, she was using the verb with an Aztec sensibility: to dis-hearten, as in to rip out someone's heart. This way, the fault lay entirely with me. My mother would end up dying from an attack on the heart, which is not the same as dying from a heart attack. She was in the National Medical Centre when part of the cardiology unit collapsed, on 19 September 1985. She was seventy-three years old and, the day before, a heart specialist from another hospital had assured her she was healthy, but she was convinced she was going to die. She kept saying she wasn't ready yet; the possibility of re-encountering my father terrified her (my father wasn't dead yet, but she didn't know this). She insisted on going to the hospital the following day to get a second opinion. As she didn't have an appointment, she went early so they'd be able to see her: she arrived before 7.19 a.m. She would have survived and lived for a few more years if only she'd paid heed to Schoenberg, whom she had obviously never read: he who doesn't seek doesn't find. But does one seek death or is it simply found?

Turnup woke up later and spent the next few hours watching the shadows that things project onto the surfaces of the world. He spent a whole afternoon observing an ant, studying its habits. Meanwhile, I was followed by someone my mother had sent, a colleague from the post office who owed her a favour, because Mum used to cover for him when he missed work. The spy managed to find out that I was going to La Esmeralda and, to jack up the value of the favour and thus clear all his debts, he told her all sorts of scandalous details, specifically that my classmates were a bunch of scruffy, gay, communist stoners. And that we'd learned all this from the finest – the teachers themselves. My mother banned me from ever going near the school again, on pain of being left an orphan, with her still alive. The same reproaches she used to hurl at my father were heard at home once more: *Art is useless. You'll starve to death. It's a luxury we can't afford.* I thought: the luxury of being an artist, or of starving to death, or the luxury of doing something useless? And as if that wasn't bad enough, the worst dig of all: *Art is for spoilt little rich kids.*

I tried to tell her about my supposed vocation, giving examples to refute what she said, made-up stories of imaginary painters who had overcome poverty and had their names carved into posterity in gilded letters.

'Don't you come to me with stories about French artists,' she interrupted. 'You're just like your father and I won't put up with it. Look at him. All he ever got from having a vocation was frustration, pure and simple. Just look how we ended up.'

Then, when I threatened to leave home, even if it was to live on the streets, to prove to her I was going to be an artist no matter how much she opposed it, she called my sister in and, with the solemnity of categorical lies, the ones there's no turning back from and which oblige those who've told them to be loyal until death, she announced that she was suffering from arthritis and that the doctor had prohibited her from working.

'I've come this far,' she said, as if her batteries had run out: 'Now it's your turn.'

From that day on, Mum devoted all her time to two things: going to the doctor and looking after her dogs. My sister got her first job as a secretary and I never returned to La Esmeralda. My adventure hadn't even lasted a year, but I had at least taken advantage of the life-drawing classes to see some naked women. Under the pretext of 'capturing their essences', I'd stared so hard at them, retaining in my mind each and every one of their folds, and had masturbated so much and so diligently that, at times of visual and carnal exhaustion, I'd reach a gloomy conclusion: the suspicion that perhaps the mystery of women was not quite so wondrous as to make it worth devoting one's life to them.

My wings clipped, I took the easiest option: I asked my uncle for work on his taco stand. Now that I had to give up my supposedly true vocation, it seemed as good a job as any; better, even, than some of the ones whose systems of slavery were so badly disguised. To be honest, perhaps being a taco seller appealed to me more because I'd developed a grudge against dogs. My uncle's stand was in the Candelaria de los Patos and he opened at night, which meant we started work at half past five. I chopped the onion and coriander, kept an eye on the tortillas, served the hibiscus tea and cinnamon rice milkshakes and gave the punters their change and a free mint. During the week the stall shut at midnight, and at the weekend, one-thirty in the morning. I gradually grew used to spending hours on my feet, going back and forth, joining in with the regular customers' banter. The only thing that annoyed me and to which I never resigned myself was the stench on my hands, my artist's hands, which now smelled of a mixture of onion, coriander, mint, sweaty notes and coins.

Tacos came and went, and I waited patiently until, early one morning, I pulled my little trick with the nylon stocking. It was my sister's, who, when she discovered in the morning that someone had been rummaging around in her chest of drawers, looked at me suspiciously until she saw Turnup lying stiff on the floor. Then she said: 'You took your time.'

To my surprise, my mother didn't request an autopsy. She went out for a walk and came back with a mutt she'd found roaming around outside the market. That's what she called him, Market, even though that wasn't even a dog's name. When my sister pointed this out, Mum refused to give him another name, playing dumb. It was something else she pretended to do around that time, as well as stopping work: pretending she didn't understand and sometimes, pretending to be mad, with no warning. Now that my sister and I were adults she seemed to have discovered that she could change the way she manipulated us, switching from her habitual intransigence, which by now was wearing thin, to an absent-minded attitude with which she gradually and heedlessly transferred to us the weight of her responsibilities.

I promised my mother I would bury Turnup and took his body to an early morning taco stand near our house. They gave me five pesos for it: the price of four beers. The next day I took her out for breakfast to cheer her up. When the taco seller saw me approach and order two tacos with everything, his hair bristled in shock, as if imagining we'd involved him in some kind of black magic ritual.

'Are they good?' I asked Mum as she chewed diligently.

With her left hand she made the sign for 'so-so' and then, once she'd swallowed her mouthful, whispered in my ear so as not to offend the stallholder: 'The meat's a bit tough.'

I went to the Chinese restaurant practically every other day to have a beer. I always took a newspaper and occasionally, my notebook. But really what I was doing was analysing the Chinese as they went back and forth, trying to figure out their secret. One day I saw them sprinkling water in the corners of the restaurant. I went back to my apartment and copied them. The cockroaches clapped their antennae together: hydrated. Another time, I wrote down in my notebook the brands of the cleaning products I saw them use, bought the same ones and gave them to the girl who came twice a week to clean the apartment, along with a series of strict instructions: apply this one neat, dilute that one with water . . . The smells changed, and the shine on the surfaces was different, too. The cockroaches, blithely unaware. I invested in some plastic plants: the cockroaches started using them as a holiday resort. I put paper shades over every light bulb, which I then had to take down again in the middle of the night: the sound of their little feet walking over them kept me awake.

I started collecting fortune cookies in a box I kept under the bed. I thought that receiving a prediction every day was excessive. Dangerous, even. Occasionally, especially when I grew desperate and was about to throw in the towel, I would open one in search of a sign, which did about as much good as a few pats on the back.

Some Wednesdays, or Saturdays, I would bring Willem along with me, and he came up with the most bizarre theories: that it was the smell of the Chinese that scared off the cockroaches. That they fried them and ate them. That the decor in the place was so horrendous that not even roaches would enter the restaurant. There was an element of truth to this last claim: the restaurant was always empty. He even bought me one of those cats with an endlessly waving little paw. A china figurine, I mean. The cat became one more ride in our cockroach theme park.

Juliet took pity on me and claimed she had a comrade who spoke Chinese, a Maoist who had learned Mandarin in Peru.

'I'll ask him to help you out,' she said, 'but you have to promise you won't ask him anything or tell anyone about him: he's undercover.'

She organised the meeting one afternoon in the shop, so she could explain the situation to him. The guy turned out to be a twenty-three-year-old kid who showed up wearing a filthy red Shining Path T-shirt. He had dreadlocks and his fingertips were stained with something that might have been ink, tobacco or gunpowder. Undercover meant that he had been living for four years in a makeshift camp run by the CAH in the faculty of philosophy at the Universidad Nacional Autónoma de México. The CAH: the Alternative Strike Council. I'd come prepared, carrying my *Aesthetic Theory*, just in case, should things start to get ugly. His eyes went straight to the book.

'Woah, Grandpa's into the hard-core stuff,' he said.

Once we'd given him the low-down on what I needed, we crossed the road and he went into the restaurant alone to talk to the Chinese. I stayed outside to wait for him. He'd said it was better that way: the Chinese love conspiracies. He came back out in less than two minutes, his face doing its best attempt (which was terrible) at imitating a patronising expression.

'Impossible,' he said. 'These Chinese are Koreans.'

He tried to charge me 200 pesos and in the end I gave him twenty. He took another look at the *Aesthetic Theory* growling in my right hand.

'If that's the kind of stuff you're into I can get more,' he assured me. 'There's a bank around here that I supply, a bank library, you know it?'

'You do business with a bank?'

'It's a postmodern form of extortion: what matters is putting capital to work in favour of the Revolution.'

'By stealing from the university?'

'The university's budget comes from the government. It's a morally right crime squared. Are you interested or not? Come on, twenty pesos a book, bargain basement!'

'I get them for free, I nick them from the library.'

'Woah! A thief stealing from a thief stealing from a thief stealing from a thief. You've earned infinite forgiveness. But in the library there is what there is, you can't choose – I'm offering you a personal delivery service.'

'Get me *Notes to Literature*.'

'Shit, only snuff films are more hard-core than that.'

'It's a present.'

'Man, well, if you put poison on the corners of the pages it's the perfect gift. I'll get it for you.'

He shook my hand in a strange fashion and our fingers got entangled. I asked him what his name was.

'Mao,' he replied.

'Your real name.'

'Mao is my real name. You know what they say, Grandpa, name is destiny.'

'Don't call me Grandpa. I'm not anybody's grandpa, I don't have grandchildren.'

'Who said you have to have grandchildren to be a grandpa? You shouldn't read so much Adorno, you'll blow a fuse.'

It was that time of the evening when people were rushing to get to the shops before they closed and which in Calle Basilia Franco could be identified by the queue in the bakery and the sound of Hipólita's pleas as she begged for crumbs among the customers. Mao had walked off nonchalantly, to the rhythm of an imaginary song, taking care to avoid the hurrying crowds. On the corner, Dorotea was waiting for him. I saw them share a long kiss and then, arm in arm, they went into the ice-cream parlour.

Willem brought me a DVD as a peace offering: a documentary about the life and work of Juan O'Gorman.

'What are you apologising for?' I asked him. 'For having betrayed me or because your convictions are stronger than our friendship?'

He thought for a minute, confused.

'You don't have to apologise,' I comforted him, 'but I am grateful for the present. Where did you buy it?'

'In the morket.'

'They're pirating documentaries on Juan O'Gorman? That really is a symbol of progress in this country. O'Gorman's my favourite.'

'I know.'

'How do you know?'

'By pay'n attention to what yuh say. To reach the Lard, yuh must learn to listen to your fellow man.'

I took the disc from its case and walked over to the machine on top of my TV.

'Hey,' I said, 'the girl from the dog police asked me about you. Want me to set you up? I'll lend you the apartment if you like, all you'd have to do is bring your own sheets.'

He flushed.

'Sex befare marriage is a sin,' he said.

'You don't say! Well, marry her then!'

On the TV screen a black-and-white photo appeared, frozen: Juan O'Gorman, his hands resting on the balustrade of a mezzanine in what appeared to be the Casa Azul. In his left hand he held a rolled-up architectural plan, in his right, a cigar. He wore a suede jacket and a pair of woollen trousers, his hair combed back and, behind his glasses, that tormented look that presaged the sadness that would befall him, if it hadn't already. Willem sensed my fascination.

'Why d'yuh like these programmes so much?'

'I've told you before: I knew all these guys, well, most of them. Some better than others, but I knew them, I could have been one of them.'

'And what happened?'

'What do you think, Villem? Not everyone achieves posterity, the world's memory wouldn't be able to remember us all, there wouldn't be enough streets to pay homage to us all, or parks to host our statues, or film-makers to make documentaries, or space for the tombs in the Rotunda of Illustrious Persons. Life has to make a selection. And it does it ruthlessly.'

'Gawd disposes.'

The TV began talking about functionalist architecture.

'God doesn't exist, my boy, it's something much more complicated, a mixture of circumstances, talent, chance, connections – genes, even! If you don't have the winning combination you end up a taco seller. And I wasn't the exception, by any means. I was the rule. How many of us who used to hang out at La Esmeralda became somebody? The minority!'

'What's La Esmeralda?'

'It's an art school. All Mexico's artistic geniuses of the twentieth century passed through its doors, either as professors or students. And the rest of us passed through, too: the cannon fodder, the filler, the extras, the gatecrashers, the ones who didn't have the combination that gives you a ticket to the history of art. We were there, the ones who one day had to renounce our aspirations, forced by circumstances or by accepting our own limitations. Then there were the ones who pressed on through mediocrity, made art their profession and condemned themselves to a life of ridicule. And on top of that were those who couldn't do anything but keep on painting, no matter what, and who ended up mad or ill, or died when they were young, martyrs of art. I knew a handful of those ones, the city's graveyards are full of them. There was one guy who had taken a few classes in La Esmeralda in the thirties and when I was studying there in 1953 he'd turn up at the gates sometimes looking for drinking buddies. I used to like the bohemian life too, so we ended up becoming friends, we were the terror of the bars in town. He showed me his paintings once, they were moving, heart-rending, brilliant. He had talent in spades, just as much as, more, even, than any of the ones who made it. Do you know what happened to him? He ended up destitute. I saw him again in 1960, at my taco stand in the Candelaria de los Patos, you know it? It's down in the centre of town. He didn't even recognise me, he was totally gone, he came to ask for some food and I gave him some tacos so he wouldn't scare my customers off. One day they found him lying in the street where my stand was. He must have been around forty. He died in the street like a stray dog.'

'What wus he called?'

'I don't even know, they used to call him the Sorcerer. I never asked him his real name and now it's impossible to find out, he was swallowed up by history. Or oblivion, rather.'

'Gawd has mercy on the fargotten ones.'

'Are you going to let me watch the film?'

Later on, after Willem finally left, I rewound the video until I spotted a photograph I'd seen out of the corner of my eye, while Willem prattled away, endeavouring to divert my attention from the screen. It was a portrait of Juan O'Gorman embracing a woman called Nina Masarov. I pressed pause and looked at the photo as I sipped my beer, then another beer, and another. Although it was a wedding photo, a postcard the artist had sent to Frida Kahlo from Europe, it was surely the saddest picture I had ever seen: to the artist's habitual tormented expression was added the resigned, absent look of the bride, who seemed to be perfectly aware that this union had no future. Or worse: that nothing had any future. I guessed she must hail from one of the superpowers of sadness: some central European country, or Germany, Poland, Mother Russia. I looked at the portrait and thought about Marilín, and about all the women who could have been mine and who never, ever were. O'Gorman was right: sometimes life was so sad you had to kill yourself three times. I'd had too much to drink. I opened my notebook and started writing down everything I remembered about Marilín, the way she growled, the length of her legs, that hair of hers she'd never let me touch, just as she never let me touch any part of her.

That night I had a dream: I was dancing a bolero with Marilín and, just as I was about to speak to her, to say one of those daft things lovers say to each other, I felt two light taps on my back. When I turned around I saw the Sorcerer holding a shoe in his right hand, an enormous great shoe he was holding up high and with which he started striking me in the face. Then everything went dark and I didn't even feel the blow as my body hit the ground. When I awoke, in the dream, I was looking up at the Sorcerer from below, I was still on the ground but we weren't in the place where I'd been dancing, we were in a bedroom. The walls of the room were covered in paintings of pigeons, dead pigeons, pigeons tied up, their feathers all plucked, their bodies bloody. There was an unmade bed, the rumpled sheets forming a tangled mass in the middle, and paintbrushes and canvases everywhere. It was the Sorcerer of the early days, with the excessive vitality of those who are unable to control the swings between joy and unhappiness, so different to the demented, emaciated Sorcerer at the end of his days. He came over to me and raised his foot, threatening to step on me, and then opened his mouth and said:

'What's going on, compadre? This novel's starting to sound really cheesy.'

'This isn't a novel,' I objected.

'Oh really! Well that's what it looks like.'

'How did we get here?'

'What does that matter?'

'We were at a dance.'

'We *were*, now we're here.'

'Where's Marilín?'

'Marilín, Marilín . . . I'VE SUFFERED MORE THAN CHRIST! YOU HEAR? I'VE SUFFERED MORE THAN CHRIST! IF YOU THINK I'M GOING TO LET YOU STICK ME IN A ROMANTIC NOVEL OR A SELF-HELP BOOK THEN YOU'RE VERY, VERY WRONG!'

At that moment I woke up, because, as well as the Sorcerer shouting in the dream, outside, in real life, I got a stabbing pain in my liver. It took me so long to get back to sleep that I memorised the whole dream.

In the morning, a tense silence in the lift as it descended. The minute the apparatus juddered to a halt in the lobby, Francesca started correcting me.

'Marilyn doesn't have an accent on the last syllable. And you spell it with a "y".'

An inspector from the Federal District department and the head of the street sellers' association came to the taco stand. It was six in the evening and my uncle hadn't arrived yet. I was standing on the corner, waiting for him. The inspector showed me his ID, making it clear that this authorised him to commit superior abuses. The other guy took out a little plastic case containing a filthy card from the National Confederation of Popular Organisations, which apparently was a passport to anywhere he could think of. I had seen this man before: he was the guy we paid our rates to. That's what my uncle called him: the rates guy. They both carried folders stuffed with papers, pens behind their ears, paper clips stuck in the buttons of their shirts; they were dressed as itinerant jobsworths.

'You're the kid who helps old Bigotes out, aren't you?' the rates guy said, inserting the card back into its plastic holder as delicately as an antiques dealer.

Bigotes was my uncle's taco-selling nickname, on account of his large moustache, and also the name of his stand: *Tacos Don Bigotes*. I said that I was and that he was running late, that by now the stand should have been set up and I should be slicing the onions and the coriander.

'Didn't you hear what happened?' the inspector asked.

I shook my head from right to left and from left to right.

'Old Bigotes kicked the bucket,' the rates guy said.

'What?' I said, from shock, but they took it to mean that I wanted to know how it had happened.

'They found him in La Alameda, he'd been stabbed five times, twice fatally,' the inspector explained.

'What?' I said again, from shock once more, and this time they thought I wanted to know why.

'Seems it was "girl trouble",' said the inspector, the tone of bureaucratic sarcasm in his voice adding scare quotes.

'Gay trouble, more like,' the rates guy said, laughing.

I raised my eyebrows as close to my hairline as I could: instinct told me it was better to pretend I knew nothing about this.

'You didn't know Bigotes was a faggot?' the inspector said.

I said that I didn't. What I actually said was: 'What?'

'What about you?' the rates guy asked.

'What about me?'

'Are you a faggot too?'

I said I wasn't, that I had a girlfriend.

'Well everyone thinks you're a faggot,' he went on. 'All Bigotes' assistants were. He brought them all from a place on Calle Luis Moya. Do you know what I'm talking about? You're not lying to us, are you?'

I explained that Bigotes had given me a job because he was my uncle. They looked at each other, as if checking whether it was appropriate to offer condolences in this kind of situation, dealing with this sort of people. They concluded that it wasn't.

'But are you a faggot or not?' the rates guy insisted.

'No, I've told you, Bigotes was my uncle.'

'Well, let's just hope it's not genetic,' the inspector said.

'Are you or aren't you?' the rates guy asked again.

I said that I wasn't, again.

'Good,' the inspector said. 'You'll be of more use to us that way.'

'Are you interested in business, kid?' the rates guy asked.

'Business?' I said, because I didn't understand, but they thought I wanted to know how it worked.

'We'll let you have this corner and you give us ten per cent of what you make,' the rates guy said. 'Ten for me and ten for my associate here.'

'Ten for the Confederation and ten for the Department,' the inspector corrected him.

'But I don't have a stand,' I said.

They explained that they'd lease it to me, that it was part of the agreement and was already included in the ten per cent.

'Twenty per cent,' the rates guy said.

'Are you in?' the inspector asked.

'I don't know, I'll have to talk to my mother.'

They looked at each other as if suspecting for a moment they'd got the wrong person and it was all a misunderstanding. They asked me how old I was. I told them I was twenty-one.

'And you have to ask your mum, kid?' the inspector said. 'What you need to do is help your mother. The stand's a really good business, you'll see.'

'Bigotes was her brother, and she doesn't know about any of this yet,' I explained.

'Even more reason not to ask her, then,' the inspector said. 'Just tell her you inherited it, she'll be happy.'

'You have to decide now,' the rates guy said. 'We're giving you an opportunity. There's a waiting list to get a spot on this corner.'

I knew it really was a good opportunity; one of the ways I used to help my uncle was by counting the money when we closed up the stand. I said yes, thinking that if I said no I'd end up with nothing, and if I accepted and I didn't like it, I could always give it up. The inspector handed me a card: on the back he'd written a code in numbers and letters.

'If one of our colleagues from the Department comes, show him this card. Keep it in your wallet. Don't lose it. Without this card you're no one, got it?'

I said yes.

'Tonight I'll come round to settle up.' The rates guy said. 'Everything had better add up, don't you try and be smart. We wouldn't want you to end up a faggot, now.'

'Another thing,' the inspector said.

He turned and looked across the road stretching out his arm to signal to a guy leaning against the wall there. The individual crossed the road without looking and a car had to screech to a halt to avoid running him down. When the driver stuck his head out of the window to curse at him, the man showed him a pistol he had hidden under his shirt, tucked into his trousers. He tucked his shirt in again and came over to where we were. He had a scar criss-crossing his face and a toothpick between his teeth. He was spectacularly ugly, like the caricature of a despot drawn by an artist troubled by the atrocities of war, so ugly it was depressing, because it implied that beauty was a moral attribute.

'Evening,' he said.

'Evening,' I repeated.

The rates guy put his right hand on the man's shoulder and informed me:

'My pal here's the one who'll sell you the meat.'

The doorbell rang and it wasn't Wednesday or Saturday. On the intercom, Mao's lilting voice announced:

'I have your order.'

'Pizza? You've got the wrong apartment.'

'I'm from the UPD: Unintelligible Philosopher Deliveries.'

I told him to come up, pressed the button that opened the main door and, in the obligatory five minutes it took him get upstairs (almost ten, as it turned out), began to imagine the commotion going on down in the lobby caused by the combination of his dreadlocks, his gently swaying walk and the pong he gave off. Finally, Mao rapped at the door to my apartment as if typing out a telegram: first one rap on its own, then several little raps spaced out and finished off with a kind of samba flourish. When I opened the door, my eyebrows expressing bewilderment, he apologised.

'It's a habit.'

I changed the position of my eyebrows to an interrogative one.

'I've been in hiding a long time.'

'You took ages, did you crawl on your knees all the way from China?'

'It's that lift, it took forever to come. I even started to think I'd miss the fall of the Yankee Empire while I was waiting.'

I let him in and he began to inspect my apartment as if he was worried I'd set up an ambush. Once he'd verified that, aside from the cockroaches, there was no one else here, he went and stood in front of the painting hanging on the wall.

'That's one cool freak,' he exclaimed.

'That's my mother,' I told him.

'And was she really that fat?'

He was wearing a Shining Path T-shirt again, which even from where he was standing gave off a stench that made clear it was the same garment. Being in hiding always was a good excuse for soap-dodgers. It suddenly occurred to me that my only visitors were militants: boys in uniform, with rucksacks on their backs.

'Hey,' he said, 'what's up with the gang in the lobby? Is it a sect?'

'Something like that. It's a literary salon.'

'Right on. And you don't take part?'

'As if! I don't read novels.'

'The novel is a bourgeois invention.'

'Oh really?'

He took off his rucksack, unzipped it and took out two books, which he handed me. I was disappointed to see that *Notes to Literature* came in two volumes and the one he had brought me, the second, was such a slim edition it might not be any use to me at all.

'What about the other volume?' I asked.

'It's gone, man, this was the only one left.'

Then I took a look at the red-and-blue cover of the other book he'd brought me: *The Dream and the Underworld*, by James Hillman.

'What's this?' I asked.

'It's a present. To bring you a bit more up to date with the latest impenetrable shit that's out there.'

I took out my wallet and gave him the agreed-on twenty pesos before I, thanks to some surprise twist in the story (including this mysterious gift), ended up having to shell out more.

'Hey, is Dorotea your girlfriend?' I asked.

'You know her?'

'Juliet introduced us. And she and I had a run-in, in any case. Did you know your little lady-friend works for the system?'

'You've got it all wrong, Grandpa.'

'I'm not confused, I saw you with her the other day. And I told you before, don't call me Grandpa.'

'But Dorotea's not who you think she is.'

'Oh, no? You're not going to tell me she's a spy?'

He sniffed, as if sniffing meant yes in the coded language of the insurgency. He sniffed again, and it seemed I'd interpreted correctly.

'My God, it's true.'

'Look, all you need to know is Dorotea's closed the file on you, you don't have to worry about that.'

'Oh really? And how much is that going to cost me? Don't think I'm going to pay you.'

'Chill, Grandpa, Dorotea's taken care of it, she's a good chick. She did it as a special favour, because you're a friend of her grandmother's.'

'And do you mind telling me what the hell you hope to achieve by infiltrating the Society for the Protection of Animals?'

'It's a gold mine of information. Have you got any idea who reports that kind of stuff? Bored, stuck-up old ladies with nothing better to do, the wives of businessmen and politicians – who else cares about animals in this country? You might laugh, Grandpa, but Dorotea just got the dope on the richest man in the world.'

'Did she really?'

'Everything: address, phone numbers, email.'

'And what are you going to do with it all?'

'I can't tell you, it'll compromise the operation.'

Then it was my turn to start looking around, as if I feared that someone else might be listening in to our conversation in my own home and I was needlessly implicating myself in who-knew-what mischief. I changed the subject abruptly.

'Did they ask you anything in the salon?'

'Man, I haven't been interrogated like this since the G-20 summit.'

'What did they ask you?'

'They asked me why I was here.'

'And what did you say?'

'That I was a supplier.'

'Brilliant. They must be thinking you're my dealer.'

'Or that I bring you your Viagra.'

'Actually, maybe you can help me out.'

'You want me to get hold of the little magic pill for you?'

'I want you to help me get hold of a whisky they make in Tlalnepantla.'

I ended up offering him a beer and later, three or four beers later, I told him to wait and went to my room, where I took the box of fortune cookies out from under the bed.

'Pick one,' I ordered him.

'Superstition is a bourgeois invention to manipula – '

'Relax, Mao, it's a tradition from your home town.'

He picked one. After opening it, he ate the cookie and put the little piece of paper in his trouser pocket.

'Well?' I asked.

'Well what?'

'What did it say?'

'I'm not telling you. If we're going to follow a tradition let's at least do it properly.'

'Eh?'

'Otherwise it won't come true.'

'It's not like it's a birthday wish. What did it say on the bit of paper?'

He put his hand back in his jeans pocket and, before fishing out the paper, removed two cables and a phone charger. Finally, he read it out:

'*Only the future gives the past a meaning.*'

'And that was what wouldn't have come true?'

'I didn't know the Chinese were revisionists.'

He put the prediction back in his pocket and, as if wanting to repay me for the beers and the cookie with a surge of indulgence, looked around into the corners of my apartment and said:

'I've got a lethal solution for roaches. Want me to bring it over?'

'Don't bother, they're invincible, they're more powerful than the Yankee army.'

'Exactly. Have you got a CD player?'

Marilín was in the same place I'd seen her last, sitting in a corner of my memory, on the edge of my bed, in my teenage fantasies, only she was still fifteen and I was an old man: women know some amazing tricks for combating the passage of time. Gingerly, I sat down next to her, trying to conceal what was going on under my fly.

'You haven't changed a bit,' I told her.

'You have.'

'I know, I'm old.'

'What year are you from?'

'2013.'

'Wow. So? Did you become an artist in the end?'

'You know I didn't.'

'I do? How could I know that?'

'We were neighbours until 1985.'

'Really?'

'Didn't you know?'

'How could I, I live in 1953.'

I gave her a stern look, thought about demanding she stop messing with me once and for all, and then I realised she was wearing her school uniform.

'So we didn't get married, then,' she said, with a sigh of relief.

'Of course we didn't.'

'Why not?'

'You're asking me?'

My outrage made her laugh out loud, satisfied that her future self had had the gall to turn me down just as she was already doing back then.

'And what happened in '85?' she wanted to know. 'Did it take you more than thirty years to lose hope?'

'My mother and my sister died and the council used the fact that the rental contract was in Mum's name to get me out of the house. I had to find somewhere else to live.'

'I'm sorry, I didn't know they'd died.'

'Yes you did, I spoke to you the day it happened.'

'So it was just mental masturbation.'

'What was?'

'Marrying me; being an artist.'

'What's wrong with masturbation?'

'You're right, I'd forgotten what a pervert you were. Just look at your trousers, they're wet already.'

At that moment, as if reality was produced by her words, I felt a dampness spread across my groin and, when I looked down to confirm the evidence of ejaculation, a shadow rose up between us suddenly, a gigantic shadow that covered everything. I looked up and saw the Sorcerer, looming menacingly – how tall was he? Sixty feet? 250? He opened his mouth to speak, or rather to shout, and it was as if he was getting ready to spit fire.

'WHAT DID I TELL YOU? WHAT DID I TELL YOU? JUST LOOK WHAT'S HAPPENING TO YOUR NOVEL. I HAVE SUFFERED MORE THAN CHRIST. I HAVE SUFFERED MORE THAN CHRIST. I HAVE SUFFERED . . . '

I woke up amid the shouting and left the warmth of my bed immediately, taking care not to fall onto the floor again. I was so shaken I even thought I heard noises in the living room. I left my bedroom and switched on the lights: there were the cockroaches, focused on their activities. I poured myself a whisky to calm myself and, as if it was an exorcism, opened my notebook and started writing furiously:

They said that María Izquierdo was afraid of him. That Juan O'Gorman liked his paintings. That Diego looked down on him from on high, scaling the arrogance of ladders and the scaffolds of his murals. That Lola Álvarez Bravo took some photographs of him that mysteriously came out blurred. That Frida didn't remember him. Or did a good job of pretending she didn't. That José Luis Cuevas didn't know if he was for him or against him. They said he came from a town where families with money diligently practised inbreeding until they overcame deformity, imbecility and madness. That he had been married twice. That he was like a seminarian who had the Devil inside him. They said he'd had smallpox, syphilis, gonorrhoea, tuberculosis, measles, parvovirus. That he used to repeat over and over again: I have suffered more than Christ, I have suffered more than Christ. *That he pretended to be from a family with money who had lost their wealth in the Cristero War. They said that Agustín Lazo told him that history's quota of tormented artists had already been filled. That he never took classes at La Esmeralda after that. They said he had schizophrenia, that he'd been committed to every single one of Mexico City's lunatic asylums, that he'd been given electroshock therapy, that he'd had a lobotomy. That he used to go to the openings of shows to scare the stuck-up old women, like someone scaring children in a park. They said his paintings looked like Giorgio de Chirico's. That he painted the landscape of the Apocalypse and that in his still lifes, the fruits made you think of necrophilia. They said he had never travelled, that he was a hick. That he'd been born in Lagos de Moreno.*

The next morning, as I left my apartment more sleep-deprived and hung-over than usual, Francesca was standing guard over the landing from her own half-open door and she yelled out:

'At last, the protagonist appears!'

A telegram had come: a wave from the Pacific Ocean had swallowed up my father. Mum didn't want to know anything and shut herself up in her room with Market. Along with a thousand other things, closed doors drove Market mad. He wouldn't stop whining; it was almost as if my mother had hired him as a professional mourner. My sister and I took a bus and, sixteen hours later, we got to Manzanillo. My father was waiting for us at the bus station. For a dead man, he looked pretty good. For a living one, abysmal.

He took us out for seafood at a little palm-covered shack by the beach. The sea smelled putrid. My father apologised, as if this, too, was his fault. We started eating our prawns and ceviche, pretending he'd never been dead. Not in reality or in our minds. Meanwhile, Dad interrogated us. Were we at university, did we have jobs. Our answers disappointed him.

'I thought you were going to be a painter,' he said to me.
'I did too,' I replied. 'I was taking classes at La Esmeralda.'
'So what happened?'
'Mum's got arthritis, I had to get a job.'
'Do you make good tacos?'
'Really good, I'm famous all over town.'

'I'm glad,' he said, with the fragile resolve of the white liar.

Then he asked me if I had a girlfriend, and I told him I was going to get married in a few months. It was the time of my supposed marriage. He asked to see a picture of my fiancée. I didn't have one on me. He asked what she was called. I told him she was called Marilín, but my sister cut in and said she was actually called Hilaria. My father tried to interrogate my sister, too, but she kept quiet, pretending to be very busy enjoying the view: she was seeing a married man on the sly. When it was time for dessert he recommended we try the mango in syrup and eventually asked us how our mother was. I enumerated her ailments for him.

We finished our dessert and it began to grow dark, and all our blood went to our stomachs to work. Then we really did have the impression we'd been eating with a ghost, that our father had died and we were in a dream. The only thing we didn't know was who was having the dream: my mother, me or my sister.

'Are you ill?' I asked him.

'I've got cancer,' he replied. 'Don't tell your mother.'

'That you're alive and you've got cancer, or that you're not dead?' my sister asked.

My father sighed, as if having cancer gave him permission to respond to reproaches by sighing and changing the subject.

'I want to ask you something,' he said. 'That's why I called you here. Can I count on you two?'

'No,' my sister said.

'It depends,' I said.

He looked at my sister one last time, before focusing on me: I knew perfectly well he'd only asked both of us so his request for help would seem like a shared burden and wouldn't weigh me down with responsibility.

'When I die,' he said, 'I want you to cremate me, mix my ashes with paint, and give them to an artist.'

It most definitely wasn't a dream, and my father wasn't dead: this kind of thing, so utterly nonsensical, only happened in real life.

'Have you gone mad?' my sister said. 'Didn't you tell us you wanted us to throw your ashes into a museum? Do you not think that's eccentric enough? Has your last screw finally come loose?'

'He's not mad,' I interrupted her. 'He's just changed his mind.'

My father looked down at the leftover mango on his plate, pre-emptively tired of having to give an explanation that at the same time was a confession of his failure.

'All I wanted to do in life,' he began, 'was to make a piece of transcendental art and I couldn't do it. I lacked talent; I lacked imagination, technique, even money. Money means time to paint, peace of mind, you can't be an artist if you have to work. But while I didn't manage to create a truly great work of art, what I can do is become one myself, become ashes stuck to a canvas, become powder paint, artistic texture.'

'I'm calling the loony bin,' my sister said.

'Son,' my father said, to exclude my sister from the conversation, 'I want you to cremate me and give my ashes to Gunther Gerzso.'

He put his right hand into his pocket and took out a piece of paper on which he'd scrawled the painter's name.

'That's not necessary,' I said. 'I know him.'

'You do?' my father asked, excited for the first time.

'I mean, I know who he is. I don't know him personally, but one of my old friends from La Esmeralda might know him. And if not him, I can probably ask José Luis Cuevas.'

'No, no, no. Cuevas is figurative, it has to be an abstract painter. The Rupture was necessary to break once and for all with muralism, you see? But that was just an intermediary phase; the trend now is towards abstractionism.'

'What about Vicente Rojo?'

'Yes, Vicente's all right. Felguérez would do, too. But try Gerzso first.'

'You're a real chip off the old block,' my sister interrupted us. 'My mother was right: you're both as frustrated as each other.'

Back at the bus station, as we said our goodbyes, my father asked if we had a dog. I told him we did.

'Watch out,' he warned us, 'you want to be careful with that.'

And then, just when it seemed like nothing else could happen, everything shifted, as if some joker had moved it all around, and suddenly there were stockings in the fridge, broken light bulbs under my pillow, the cockroaches were reading Proust, the dead grew tired of being dead and the past was no longer what it had been.

NOTES TO LITERATURE

The incident was front-page news in all the papers, the radio was repeating it over and over and it was the main item on all the TV bulletins that day: the ground around the esplanade to the Monument to the Revolution was cracking. There were thousands of jokes on the internet about it, photomontages showing a dinosaur bursting up out of the ground. Juliet showed me some of them on her phone. We'd missed our chance to go and desecrate Madero's tomb – we were about to head over there but the area had been cordoned off. Two days later, the experts appointed to find an explanation delivered their verdict and the dinosaur story suddenly seemed tame. It was the Revolutionaries' moustaches, which hadn't stopped growing and had got all tangled up in the sewer system. The experts' assessment was so exact it set out who was responsible: the fault lay with Villa and Cárdenas. Madero, Calles and Carranza were absolved.

I copied down in my notebook the conversations I had over those days with Juliet, all our speculations, to make Francesca jealous.

'The Revolution's really coming this time,' Juliet announced, beaming. 'It's just like in '85! People here only wake up when the ground opens up under their feet.'

'Don't be ridiculous, *Juliette*,' I countered. 'All that's going to happen is they'll change the names of a few streets, take down a few statues. Just look at who they're blaming! If the Monument falls down completely they'll say that Pancho Villa and Lázaro Cárdenas were terrorists.'

'The people won't let themselves be manipulated now, Teo, you'll see: when the underground's involved the gods of death and destruction all rise up, the monsters from the subsoil. Think about 1985. It took an earthquake swallowing part of Mexico City, thousands of deaths for people to wake up. Just like now. They're waking up Coatlicue, our mother of the subsoil! You know who that is?'

'Of course I do, she's Huitzilopochtli's mother.'

'Our temple-sweeping mother, miraculously impregnated like the Virgin Mary, except by a little ball of feathers instead of a dove, and who forms with her son a duality: darkness and light, waste and fertility, death and life. Do you know what happened when they found the figure of Coatlicue that's in the Anthropology Museum now? They put her back in the ground! And not just because they were frightened by such a terrible image – this was in 1790 and the Church ordered that it be buried again because they were worried about the influence it might have on young people. If they hadn't put her back I guarantee Coatlicue would have speeded up the start of Independence by twenty years!'

'Coatlicue my arse! Young people nowadays don't know anything about Aztec mythology.'

'That doesn't matter, you don't need to know it, we all carry it inside us. And anyway, who said it's young people who are going to start the Revolution? What if we're the ones who have to do it? We've got nothing to lose, we've barely got any future left.'

'But we've got a lot of past. Don't kid yourself, *Juliette*, the only ones who've got nothing to lose are the dead.'

'Or the living dead.'

In the lift, I don't recall whether going up or going down, Francesca harangued me furiously: 'This is plagiarism! I think it's from a novel by García Márquez, except he has a woman's hair that won't stop growing, not moustaches.'

'Really! And do you consider it plagiarism when reality starts imitating a novel? Run and tell the experts who wrote the report: if they sue a Nobel Prize-winner it's going to cost them an arm and a leg!'

Papaya-Head stuck his papaya head into the bar on the corner, where I was on beer number six. It was barely two in the afternoon but as it was a Sunday I was working, earnestly and resolutely, to earn my weekly bread: free bar snacks. He walked over to the table where I was sitting alone, and I could almost see him spitting out the black, gelatinous papaya seeds, except it was only spittle.

'They said I'd find you here.'

'They were right. You'll find me here from nine until two and from four till eight Monday to Friday, and I'm also on duty weekends. You work on Sundays too?'

'I'm not here on business. Can I sit down?'

'Can I say no? What are you drinking? Tequila, mezcal? Or would you prefer something stronger?'

'Stronger?'

'Caustic soda, chlorine, turps . . . '

'I'll have a beer.'

I shouted at the barman to bring us a large bottle of Corona and concentrated on trying to figure out why Papaya-Head would go around wearing such an extravagant combination of colours: a fluorescent yellow T-shirt with orange Bermuda shorts, a tropical kind of get-up, the opposite to the grey suit he'd been wearing when he'd visited me as a representative of the dog police. Did he know his head looked like a papaya?

'You should be at the beach in that,' I said. 'Nice T-shirt, perfect for hiding from a sniper.'

'It was a present.'

Which I interpreted as: his wife was the one who, consciously or not, bought his clothes for him in accordance with the shape of his head.

'Did your wife give it to you?' I asked.

'Something like that,' he replied.

'Does "something like that" mean a girlfriend, a mistress?'

'"Something like that" means something like that.'

Our beer arrived and I poured out two glasses; Papaya-Head immediately took a loud gulp. Without the formal protocols of work, which covered up his social awkwardness, what remained was a civilised, twenty-miles-an-hour car crash, not at all fatal, but irritating nonetheless.

'I want to ask for your help,' he said.

'Do you now! Let's drink a toast first, though.'

I held my glass of beer up towards the centre of the table.

'To dogs!' I exclaimed.

'Hey, that report was archived,' he said, bristling.

'I know it was, but that was all Dorotea's doing.'

'And it was totally illegal, it violated all the procedures of the Society for the Protection of Animals and I could revoke it at any moment if I wanted.'

'Are you threatening me?'

'No, I'm asking you for help.'

I was worried that Papaya-Head had found out Dorotea was an undercover agent in the Society for the Protection of Animals and that now, taking advantage of my friendship with

Juliet, he had come to ask me to infiltrate the group that had organised the infiltration. This worry, which rose up rapidly like a pang of paranoia in my liver, was substituted just as rapidly for horror, when Papaya-Head announced:

'I want to write a novel.'

'You don't!'

I looked straight into his eyes, the pupils a dull brown like the bruises on a papaya just past its best, and there I verified that, unfortunately, there was no spark of a joke or a lie in them.

'It's more serious than I thought,' I said. 'We're going to need something stronger.'

I raised my right arm to call the waiter over, like in school when you ask permission to go to the toilet, an angle twenty degrees off a fascist salute, and shouted out my order: 'Two tequilas! Urgently!'

I tried to stop seeing the papaya in the papaya-shaped head of Papaya-Head and started analysing the tautness of the peel of his face, the weariness of his gaze, the nature of the expression formed by the outermost folds of his lips, closer to melancholy than sarcasm, and miles away from cynicism, in order to calculate his age. He was around forty. Perhaps he was thirty-nine, and this tale about writing a novel was nothing more than a manifestation, albeit a quaint one, of a midlife crisis, particularly serious in the case of papayas.

'How old are you?' I asked.

'Thirty-nine.'

I knew it! I recalled that in the mid '70s, it had hit me very hard: I'd rented an apartment I never moved into, I'd proposed to a hooker on Calle Madero, I'd thought I had cancer and, in a moment of madness, I'd bought a load of canvases which then sat stacked on top of a wardrobe in my mother's house, which

I hadn't moved out of because I didn't have enough money left to buy the paint or the brushes, never mind to actually start painting or stop believing I was a substitute for my father. Or to really believe it and do the same thing he'd done all those years before: abandon my family. My inner turmoil had, at least, been the necessary crucible for the inspiration of my 'Gringo Dog' recipe, the taco filling that had made me famous in the eighties. But it was one thing to invent a taco filling and quite another to write a novel, so I hastily started trying to discourage Papaya-Head. Better to kill off a novel now before it intoxicated a hopelessly hopeful author than to condemn ourselves to the torture it would be, for him, to write it, and for me, to have to read it.

'Now listen here,' I said, employing my best pedagogical tone, a mishmash of pity, indulgence, weariness and the useless superiority we elderly folk insist on believing we have over the young. 'I've already told you I'm not writing a novel. You shouldn't listen to my neighbours, they've got too much time on their hands – they spend their whole lives gossiping and, besides, they read far too many books. You don't understand this yet because you're still young, but at our age people make things up not because they have to or as some kind of strategy, they do it just because, for the fun of it, they invent stuff so as to tangle things up and so they then have to untangle them afterwards. Untangling tangles is very entertaining, that's how we spend our time.'

'I know you're writing a novel,' he replied, as if papayas didn't have ears. 'You're forgetting I found the proof in your apartment.'

I arched my eyebrows up, halfway between the well-worn path that leads from incomprehension to misunderstanding.

Since he failed to comprehend, I had to translate my expression into a question.

'What are you talking about?'

'The notebooks! What else?'

I sighed, or huffed, or puffed, or a bit of all three at once, before contradicting him.

'That's not a novel, they're drawings, notes, things that occur to me; I write them down out of sheer boredom. You're young, you don't need to write things down, life is out there, the world's your oyster.'

'If it wasn't a novel, you'd have let me see the notebooks,' he reasoned.

He knocked back the last of his tequila, ignoring my soothing speech and taking as a given what he'd already decided: that I was lying.

'Let me tell you about the story I've thought of,' he said. 'It's a detective novel. It's about a serial dog-killer, he works in pest control, actually, and he has a business supplying every taco stand in Mexico City. It's inspired by a real case I dealt with in my job, a butcher's that used to supply dog meat to taco stands.'

'Well I never.'

'They'd been doing it for years and we managed to expose them, we put the owner in jail and tightened up the health and safety inspection procedures in butchers' shops.'

'Now I understand.'

'What?'

'Why tacos have been so bad recently.'

He picked up his glass of beer and slurped noisily, trying to show me he was coming to the end of his tether.

'Why do you insist on playing the fool?' he said. 'You're like a little child.'

'Only to convince you that I can't help you write your novel.'

'You're the perfect person, not only because you know how to write a novel, but because you were a taco seller too.'

'And what's that got to do with it?'

'I'm going to write the novel from the point of view of a taco seller.'

'I wasn't a taco seller.'

'You told the butcher you were! It's all in the report! Or have you forgotten already that you tried to sell a dog to the butcher around the corner? Why do you think they assigned me to your case? I'm an expert in the illegal dog-meat trade.'

It was this sort of thing that made me feel like I'd been born in the previous century, a twentieth century that was looking more and more like the nineteenth century; this was the bewilderment that led me to call for drinks at shorter and shorter intervals in bars, that meant my whisky ran out sooner than I'd anticipated, the bewilderment that was diminishing my savings and which, day by day, was cutting short my life.

'What harm will it do you to help me write a novel?' Papaya-Head insisted in a conciliatory tone, picking up on my consternation. 'If you help me I promise that report won't cause you any problems. If you refuse I'll destroy the medical certificate Dorotea got hold of, the one that says you're an alcoholic suffering from dementia, and if I do that the report will be active again. By the way, do you have any idea what sort of punishment you'd receive?'

'The electric chair?'

'It's quite a hefty fine.'

He then pronounced an astronomical figure, an amount of money I'd be able to live on for three years, if I was careful, or two, if I continued at the present rate. My life shortened by two or three years!

'That's the minimum,' he added, 'and, I assure you, you wouldn't get away with it. Do you realise who the man who filed the complaint is? He's a very influential person.'

'So influential that when he realises the case has been closed he can force you to open it again?'

'The trick is to palm them off until they get bored; people like this get bored quickly. But if the case is open and it progresses, you can be sure they'll have no qualms about bringing you to justice.'

I necked my tequila in one to try and forget that a quarter of my savings might soon line the pockets of the richest man in the world and his family. And worst of all: to atone for my supposed role in their misery.

'Where shall we start?' said Papaya-Head.

I made one last, desperate attempt.

'Aren't you ashamed to blackmail an old man?'

'You want my pity? You don't want anyone's pity.'

'Don't try and psychoanalyse me. Do you at least know how to write? What did you study?'

'Veterinary science.'

'And you want to write a novel?'

'I told you already: I don't know how to write a novel, but I've got the most important thing.'

I raised my eyebrows into an obvious question mark, with no room for misinterpretation.

'Experience,' he said.

'There are writing workshops,' I suggested.

'At impossible times for me. I can only go on Sundays, at this time.'

'Don't you have to see to your wife and kids on Sundays?'

'I told you, I don't have a family.'

'You didn't tell me anything, all you did was mention a mysterious "something like that". Maybe you're bent? It wouldn't matter, it might even work in your favour, there're tons of gay writers.'

'That's prejudice.'

'You're wrong, *0 writer*, that's statistics.'

He fell silent, his silence consenting for him. Then he returned to the only topic that interested him:

'Shall we start next Sunday?'

'I guess there's nothing for it.'

'Do I need to bring anything?'

'It's a writing workshop, not a knitting class.'

'But I ought to bring something, right? Material to work on, I don't know.'

'Bring a ball of wool.'

'Eh?'

'Bring along what you've got of your novel, I mean.'

Before he left, three large bottles of beer and two tequilas later, my tongue and attitude looser, and feeling wildly impertinent (as well as content, because Papaya-Head had paid for every round), I asked him:

'Hey, don't take this the wrong way, but has anyone ever told you your head looks like a papaya?'

'You're confusing me with someone else,' he replied, amused, with the deceptive, false camaraderie brought on only by tequila. 'That's my brother.'

'Your brother?'

'Yeah, my older brother, everyone calls him The Big Papaya.'

My sister had announced she had a new job: she was going to be a secretary at a dog-food factory. It wasn't one of life's little ironies; her boss had switched companies and was taking her with him, as a reward for her supposed efficiency. My mother was about to say: Well he's obviously got the wrong end of the stick. Before she could, my sister announced she'd be getting a discount on dog biscuits. Mum wanted to know how much. Fifty per cent, my sister replied. My mother said it was still extortionate considering Market ate our leftovers, which didn't cost a thing, following the principle that there was always room for one more at the dining table, especially if one of the extra diners was a dog. Back then, towards the end of the fifties, dog biscuits were a novelty and a source of great wonderment as they seemed so modern: if a handful of dry cereals could fulfil all the needs of an animal, it was as though dogs had suddenly become more advanced than humans, who still had to resort to all sorts of complicated recipes. My sister said that Market's breath stank (this was true) and that the biscuits would put an end to it. My mother said nothing, because the truth was that up to now the mutt's foul-smelling mouth had prevented her from growing fond of him. Actually, she did say something. She said:

'Well, we'll see.'

Which meant that she accepted my sister's new job and would put her suspicions aside while we tested the effect of the biscuits on the dog.

My sister began bringing sacks of dog food home, one a fortnight. And, just as she'd said, not only did Market's breath stop smelling but his coat turned all silky and shiny. All our neighbours wanted to stroke the animal, which became the most handsome specimen on the block. My mother was over the moon.

Until one day, Market started choking at dinner time. Miraculously, he didn't die. Miraculously – and because Mum stuck her fingers down his windpipe, from where she rescued a piece of paper, folded up small. An obscene message that had been deposited there for my sister, inside the bag of dog biscuits. It said – I can still remember it – among declarations of a forbidden love: *your legs are longer than the road to Cuernavaca.* And: *your curves are like the ones on the road to Puerto Vallarta.* The company my sister and her boss used to work for provided services to the Ministry of Communications and Transport. It could have been worse: had the new job made similar inroads in her boss's imagination, his similes could have been further enriched. It was all written in red ink on a sheet of the company's headed notepaper.

Mum shut herself up in her room with Market, who wouldn't stop whining, as if he foresaw a return to a diet of rice, stale tortillas, beans and old bones. She emerged later, as if nothing had happened, and no one spoke of the matter again. There were no punishments, no demands, no prohibitions; there was silence, and something new that came with adult life: pretence. There was too much suffering in the family as it was to go and ruin the dog's coat as well.

I had been flicking through my Hillman, reading fragments here and there like a chicken pecking randomly, and without even looking I'd come across an oh-so-long, oh-so-fat, succulent worm. I copied the phrase into my notebook with all the bad intentions in the world: *As truths are the fictions of the rational, so fictions are the truths of the imaginal.* The hermeneutical skirmish in the salon lasted a week. Just as they were about to come to an agreement about what they all thought they'd understood, I walked through the lobby, as if by chance, and dropped this bombshell on them:

'You're confusing the imaginal with the imaginary. They're two different things. The imaginary is merely reproductive, while the imaginal has a productive power, as an organ of knowledge.'

I'd learned it off by heart, it was on page 59. They were so perplexed that they went back to their *Lost Times* and put the argument on the back-burner for a couple of days, while their stomachs digested the sticky mess. Then they returned to the fray. Francesca was the first to reach a conclusion, which she rubbed my nose in one morning while we went down in the lift together.

'I've got half a mind to think you're suffering from delirium tremens.'

'Oh really!'

'Productive fictions only happen when you're hallucinating. Perhaps if you didn't drink so much . . . '

'How little you've lived, *Frrrancesca*, that's your problem. Perhaps if you didn't read so much . . . '

I ended up giving Hillman's book to Juliet, who I thought would appreciate his revolutionary theories about the underworld. As the beers came and went I presented her with it and, in order to head off her surprise at the gift, I read her the phrase that had made me think of her: *the underworld is the mythological style of describing a psychological cosmos.*

'Well thank you, Teo,' she said, 'but next time you could at least give me something written in Spanish.'

'It's just what you said the other day,' I replied.

'Oh Lord, how many had I had?'

'This explains the earthquake in '85, and the crack in the Monument to the Revolution.'

'Well it explains it so badly you're going to have to explain it to me again.'

'What it's saying is that there's a connection between mythology and the psychology of the masses. When the earth cracks open, the mythological gods wake up in people's minds and they rebel. It's exactly what you said the other day!'

'Are you accusing me of being intellectual?'

'I'm accusing you of being intelligent.'

In return, softened more by the gesture than the gift itself or the compliment, Juliet announced she was going to show me her treasures. She invited me to come into her room, at the back of the shop. I said I'd swing by the pharmacy first and that we'd have to wait a little while for the magic to take effect.

'You really are a clown, Teo,' she said.

Out the back of the shop there was a little patio and then a little further on, her bedroom, with no windows or ventilation, like a cave. Inside, the bed and all the junk you could possibly imagine and possibly fit into thirty square feet. Juliet turned on a lamp with a white light that dazzled all the cockroaches, who ran to hide behind or beneath the knick-knacks. From inside a trunk she took out two delicate little glass boxes. The first one she handed to me contained a transparent flake, of an orangey colour, stuck to what I supposed was the lower part. I stood and observed all four sides of the thing. All six: from above and below, too. I had no idea what it might be, if it still was something. Or what it had been, if it had ceased to be it. Or even what it might come to be, in the event it was growing, evolving, changing. And I had even less of an idea why it was in a little glass box and Juliet considered it a treasure. I told her I was going to step out onto the patio to look at it in daylight.

'Relax,' she said. 'I know you've got no idea what it is. It's not a riddle. It's a tomato, a tomato from 1988. This tomato touched our engineer Cuauhtémoc Cárdenas Solórzano on the sixteenth of July. Remember that day? The earthquake of '85 had a deadly aftershock: a tremor in society. That was the day the Revolution was going to start. It was going to, but the Engineer stopped it. People were itching to take the National Palace and he calmed us all down. He said no, no, no. Was he prudent, as history records, or had he made a pact with the government? What do you think?'

She held the other box out to me, and here it was easier to make out that the contents had once been a tomato, not just by comparing it to the previous one, but because it hadn't yet been reduced to a flake: it had been a tomato in more recent times.

'This one's from 2006,' the greengrocer said. 'Do you know how many people there were in the Zócalo on that day? Over a million, they say. Can you imagine what would have happened if López Obrador had said the right words? He forgot to finish off that phrase about "to hell with institutions". Crowds can't start interpreting things – crowds, like armies, need orders. Another lost opportunity.'

I gave her back the little glass boxes. Juliet returned them to the trunk, where they would continue their progress towards total volatilisation. For a second I thought she was now going to show me her real treasure: an arsenal.

'Do you know why I've kept these tomatoes?'

'To remember,' I replied.

'Not to forget,' she corrected me.

Hanging from the wall I discovered a photo in a little wooden frame, old yet polished. It was a newspaper clipping showing the faces of four young men: one was talking into a slender microphone held in his right hand, the two flanking him were staring off into the distance and, behind them, a dark-skinned guy with a moustache, his chin in his hand, stared intently at the one who was speaking. Judging by their hairstyles, the frame on the glasses worn by the one holding the mike, their shirt collars and their jacket lapels, I calculated it must be a photo from the sixties.

'Now you must think I'm bonkers,' Juliet said.

I said that I was actually thinking she was a soppy old thing. I went over to the wall to read what was written beneath the photo: 'Press conference called last night in the faculty of philosophy at the Universidad Nacional Autónoma de México, by the National Strike Council.'

'The guy with the moustache is my brother,' Juliet said. 'Do you know where he is now?'

I guessed he was undercover. Or I tried to guess, but I didn't say anything out loud, naturally. Instead, I raised my eyebrows, forming a question.

'If only I knew,' she explained. 'He went missing thirty-five years ago.'

I looked at the photo again, carefully this time. Juliet's brother was the only one who looked convinced he wanted to be there; the other three were already fleeing, at least in spirit.

'Do you have siblings?' she asked me.

'I had a sister, but she died.'

'Was she older than you?'

'A year older.'

'How did she die?'

'In the earthquake of '85. And my mother, too.'

'Seriously? Why didn't you ever tell me?'

'I don't like thinking about it. You've never told me about your brother, either.'

'Where did the tremor hit?'

'The cardiology ward.'

'You're not making this up, are you?'

'As if.'

'I don't know, we're so close to the bed.'

'Pity's a terrible seduction technique.'

'You'd be surprised, it can work.'

'Seriously?'

'But not with me. Shall we have a mezcal?'

'Or a couple, even.'

We left her bedroom and went back through the shop as I mused that this was what being undercover really meant: two unburied bodies, the living dead, the ones who are alive only through a trick, or a crack that suddenly appears in one's memory.

One afternoon, on a day that could have been any of those days that followed mercilessly on from each other (except Wednesday or Saturday as Willem hadn't come earlier and would not come later), the crunching of metal outside announced that two cars had had a crash. I went out onto the balcony and, among the gossiping crowds, saw the entire literary salon striding over to the site of the accident. I downed what was left of my beer and, carrying my copy of *Aesthetic Theory* to create yet more confusion, headed downstairs with a view to joining the fray.

In the lobby, the copies of *In Search of Lost Time* lay face down, abandoned on the chairs with their legs spread open. I opened the *Aesthetic Theory*'s legs and placed it on top of one of the *Lost Times*, face down. It was things like this that at times made me wonder whether it might not be a bad idea to stop drinking, or at least to cut back a little. I went over to Francesca's throne, the chair that presided over the circle, positioned at an angle from which she could observe both the lift and the main door. I hefted the brick up to within sight of my failing eyes, turned on the little light, used the magnifying glass to focus, and read:

However disillusioned we may be about women, however we may regard the possession of even the most divergent types as an invariable and monotonous experience, every detail of which is known and can be described in advance, it still becomes a fresh and stimulating pleasure if the women concerned be – or be thought to be – so difficult as to oblige us to base our attack upon some unrehearsed incident in our relations with them . . .

The salon members were a bunch of wanton hypocrites. I looked around and found a red pen, which I used to underline the passage. In the left-hand margin of the page, and along the top, because the message wouldn't fit, I wrote: *Exactly! Are you going to let me give you one or just carry on being a prim old prick-tease?*

This done, my plans changed. I went back up to my apartment, poured myself a glass of beer and settled myself into the Corona chair on the balcony to wait for the moment when the salon returned. It took them about twenty minutes, which was the time it took for an ambulance to arrive and take away one of the drivers, who'd broken a leg (I only learned this later, when Juliet told me). Just as they walked under my balcony, I shouted:

'Went out to give your piles an airing, did you?'

Once they'd disappeared from view and were back in the lobby, I counted the seconds and didn't even get to thirty. Francesca appeared out on the pavement again and, lifting her flushed and furious face up at the balcony, screamed: 'You brute!'

'You forgot the mariachi band!'

'Pervert!'

'Me? I'm not the one reading smutty books!'

'It's literature!'

'Oh, well you should have said so!'

'Come down and read it if you're so brave!'

'Why don't you come up here? Forget about literature, let's try experience for a change!'

She stuck her tongue out, blew a raspberry and went back into the building. I went to the fridge to get another beer, smug and content as you like, whistling 'Ode to Joy', when the disaster dawned on me: I'd left my *Aesthetic Theory* in the lobby. I ricocheted downstairs like a frantic firework, trapped in the elevator's exasperating slowness, and burst into the lobby shouting:

'Hands up! Nobody move!'

Against her nature, Francesca kept her mouth shut, and the obedient, passive stance did not bode well. By now it was almost night and, in the darkness, the salon with its little lights looked like a group of miners exploring a cave. I located the chair where I remembered, or thought I remembered, having left the *Aesthetic Theory* with its legs open: Hipólita's seat. As I went over to her she shyly removed her glasses, the cast on her right hand accentuating her usual clumsiness, and placed them in her lap with exaggerated care, as if they were a tiny bird whose bones she was trying not to crush.

'Good evening, Hipólita,' I said.

'Night,' she replied. 'Wood night.'

The painkillers were now causing linguistic disorders of the most creative sort.

'Would you be so kind as to give me back the book I left on top of your *Lost Time*?'

She looked over at Francesca, asking for help, and with her left hand nervously squeezed her glasses, almost crushing the tiny bird. Francesca was undaunted and ordered Hipólita to resist with an imperceptible movement of her eyebrows; imperceptible, that is, to those who are not experts in the semiotics of the supercilium.

'I don't know what you're squawking about,' she replied.

The dictator was wielding admirable control over the salon, capable even of imposing her will over that of a highly powerful drug. I looked around me, at the other salon flunkies, who were pretending this was nothing to do with them, and they were right: it was never to do with them. Idly, I looked underneath the chairs, on top of the letter boxes, in every corner of the lobby, knowing even as I did so that I wasn't going to find anything.

'So this is what it's come to, is it?' I exclaimed. 'If you want war you'd better be ready for it.'

Francesca, who'd been holding back so as to carry out her satanic plan, replied: 'Hipólita's already told you we don't know what you're talking about. It's not our problem you've lost your book. Perhaps if you didn't drink so much . . . '

'If I didn't drink so much you wouldn't be such a bunch of thieves?'

'If you didn't drink so much you wouldn't have lost your book. Look for it, but see that you look hard. He who doesn't seek does not find.'

Since I didn't know what love was, I confused it with an elevator that went up and down between my legs, powered, complete with a remote control, by Marilín's voice during our chats. On the long tram journey back home from Coyoacán I was doomed to suffer one of two calamities, both equally humiliating: testicular pain, or getting my trousers all wet.

'What did you do?' I asked her.

'I posed,' she replied.

'Nude?'

'What do you think? You men are all the same.'

'Nothing else? You didn't do anything else?'

'What else would I do? What have you been imagining?'

'And what's he doing, a painting?'

'Sketches, he says they're studies for a mural.'

I was barred from whatever was going on inside the house, in the studio, despite the fact that Marilín's mother had given her permission only on the condition that I accompany her daughter at all times. When we got there, the door to the house would open and, without fail, Diego Rivera's brilliant hand, the same hand with which he commanded the history of art in Mexico, would hand me a peso and order me to come back in two hours. I would leave and walk around the block, but I came back immediately and stationed myself across the road trying to get a glimpse of something through a half-open window, watching people coming and going from the house, a stream of characters that made one imagine all sorts of conspiracies. More than once, my suspect presence attracted the attention of the police, who assumed I must be planning some kind of atrocity. Until at last, two and a half, three hours later, never the promised two, the door would open and Marilín would cross the threshold that returned her to the street, to the tram and to my questions:

'What did you do?'

'You know what – I posed.'

'Naked?'

'What do you think? Does it turn you on, Teo?'

'I'd rather you didn't go.'

'Oh really! You're far too pushy, if Frida heard you she'd castrate you for sure.'

'Frida? Who's Frida?'

'What do you mean, who's Frida? She's Diego's wife.'

The tram continued on its way, and when finally we reached our neighbourhood, I'd ask her: 'Are you going to let me draw you?'

'Tomorrow.'

I began carrying my sketchbook with me, hoping to show it to Diego one day to ask his advice, and also to keep myself occupied as I waited for Marilín. When the door opened, I'd hold out my pad to Diego and the door would slam in my face, in my ridiculous potato-nose, I mean. As the days came and went, one of the regular visitors to the house, a man who wore a pair of very sad spectacles, came over one afternoon to where I was standing.

'It's not the first time I've seen you loitering here,' he said. 'Mind telling me what you're up to?'

'I'm drawing,' I replied.

'Out on the street?'

'I'm waiting for a friend of mine who's in there.'

'Marilín's a friend of yours?'

'Yes.'

'A friend or a girlfriend?'

'A friend. Are you a painter too?'

His face twisted into an expression that meant neither yes nor no, rather that the question was impertinent.

'I'm the architect of the house,' he said.

'But you're a painter too, aren't you?' I insisted.

He agreed that he was with an affirmative movement of his sad glasses.

'Could you take a look at my drawings and give me some advice?' I begged him.

I handed him my sketchbook, where there was an outline of the house and a whole load of sketches of Marilín's face in profile, which I drew on the tram, as she posed, involuntarily, and whispered into my ear: 'Does it turn you on, Teo?'

And I did get wet. Perhaps the man with the sorry glasses would be able to see what was behind these portraits, my sorry pursuit without end or hope. After carefully leafing through the book, he raised the sadness that was his glasses, closed the pad and gave it back to me.

'How old are you?' he asked.

I told him I was nearly eighteen, although in reality I had just turned sixteen.

'Have you ever taken drawing classes?'

I said I hadn't.

'So you like the girl, eh?' he said.

'Can you tell from the drawings?' I asked.

'You can, from the number of times you've drawn her.'

'What do you think?'

'I think you lack technique, but that can be learned. Go to La Esmeralda.'

'What's that?'

'It's an art school.'

He grabbed the sketchbook from me, selected a blank page at random and, leaning against the wall, started writing with a pen he took from the pocket of his overcoat, an overcoat too heavy for the warm weather at the time.

'Where is the school?'

'On Callejón de la Esmeralda.'

He gave me back the notebook and took his leave, saying: 'Don't hang around here; the police will think you're a thief, and some of Diego and Frida's friends will get nervous. Go and take a walk, or else you'll end up a model too with that nose of yours, only for a still life.'

I watched his melancholy walk as he left and, when he had gone far enough so he couldn't see my reaction to his note, I read what he'd written in my sketch pad:

To the Directors of the National School of Painting, Sculpture and Engraving, La Esmeralda: I hereby request that the boy bearing this letter be enrolled in life-drawing classes. He might well learn how to hold a pencil, or at the very least get to see a naked woman.

    Yours faithfully, Juan O'Gorman.

I had stayed in my apartment, monitoring things from the balcony, until at last I had seen the procession of salon members, led by Francesca, leave the building and head for the Jardín de Epicuro. Then I initiated the operation to recover my *Aesthetic Theory*. I crossed the twelve feet separating my door from Francesca's and, into the crack, inserted my ID card from the National Institute of Senescence, which last year had changed its name to the National Institute of Mature Adults but I hadn't got a new card yet. It took me two seconds to hear the click that announced the opening of the door; it was something I'd had to do more than once, after locking myself out. On these occasions, when she came across me fiddling with my door, Francesca would accuse me: 'Perhaps if you didn't drink so much . . . '

'If I didn't drink so much the locks on doors would be impossible to pick?'

I pushed the door and at that moment the shrill noise of the alarm rang out, which, as well as giving me palpitations for a couple of hours, meant I was obliged to put a few drops of painkiller into my ears. I shut the door and went back to my apartment as fast as I could. The alarm shut itself off two minutes later. All I managed to see, through the half-open door, was a poster of Octavio Paz hanging from the living-room wall.

I was debating with Willem about what dead people would look like when they came back to life, on Judgement Day: would they really rise up from under the ground, covered in soil, half-rotten, or would they materialise immaculate, translucent, incorporeal, like a spiritual presence?

'Just imagine, Villem,' I said. 'Everyone who's ever died in the history of humanity – how many do you reckon there are – thousands of millions, surely? Think of them all suddenly above ground, some just skeletons, others with bits of rotting flesh hanging off them, all covered in maggots, and as if that wasn't enough, the huge great cloud of ashes from the ones who were cremated; the Bible's such a gruesome book!'

'It won't happen like that,' Willem replied. 'The Bible isn't meant to be interperted that closely.'

'Look who's talking! Of course it'll be like that, that's what it's like in films and when it comes to the living dead the cinema has always used the Bible as a guide.'

'Felms are very often sinful.'

'Oh really!'

Just then the intercom buzzed and interrupted our disquisitions. I picked up the receiver and heard Mao's voice.

'I've come from the TCF.'

'The Twisted Consumerist Federation?'

'The Trotskyist Cockroach Fumigators.'

'You can start in the lobby, it's crawling with literary pests.'

'You got it.'

'Come on up.'

Willem put his Bible (in which he'd been consulting passages on the Apocalypse) back in his rucksack, and asked:

'Wouldyuh like me to go?'

'No, stay,' I replied. 'It's a friend of mine, you'll like him.'

We positioned ourselves to wait for Mao to appear but since, as usual, he took ages to arrive, Willem took his Bible out again and started going after cockroaches. Ever since the *Aesthetic Theory* had been kidnapped, the cockroaches were proliferating merrily; I had tried to reduce their numbers with *Notes to Literature*, but the book was very slight and no matter how hard I thwacked the creatures I only left them stunned. Finally Mao rapped out the entry code on the door with his knuckles. I opened it and saw that Dorotea was with him. I raised my eyebrows mischievously.

'If you want to use my apartment,' I informed him, 'you need to let me know in advance, and you've got to bring your own sheets. Besides, I've got company. But come on in, I think your girlfriend wanted to meet my pal here.'

They crossed the threshold and as soon as Mao detected Willem's presence he stepped back as if heading for the door again.

'Is this an ambush?' he asked.

'Exactly,' I said. 'Organised by Jesus Christ.'

'I'm serious,' Mao insisted: 'Everyone knows the Mormons work for the CIA.'

'Relax, Mao,' I told him. 'My friend Villem here says that spying's a sin.'

Mao looked at him as he whacked his Bible against the wall to squash a cockroach. A sarcastic expression appeared on his face, interpreting – erroneously – that using the word of God as a bug-killer was an act of heterodoxy that at least merited the benefit of the doubt.

'Spyin' is a sin,' Willem confirmed, as he wiped the cover of his Bible off with a piece of toilet paper.

'And it's not a sin to use the Bible to squash cockroaches?' Mao asked. 'Isn't it a sin to kill little animals?'

'Cockroaches are the Devel's beasts,' said Willem. 'The word of the Lard is very firm about the Devel.'

Dorotea went over to Willem and held out her hand, unsure whether to greet him with a kiss or not. Willem's hands were full and in his confusion he ended up stuffing the toilet paper containing the remains of the cockroach into his trouser pocket.

'Hello, Willem, how are you doing?' Dorotea said.

'You know each other?' Mao interrupted.

'They met the other day,' I put in, 'when your girlfriend came to accuse me and my friend here used his visit to betray me.'

What with Dorotea hesitating and Willem growing more awkward, instead of kissing hello they had ended up with their hands intertwined, gently moving them up and down.

'Are you going to let go of her hand, buddy?' Mao said, in English.

'Calm down, comrade,' I said. 'So much revolution and clandestine activity and all to end up acting like a guy in a telenovela. What have you brought me? I warn you, Villem's tried everything and just look around, the roaches are happy as Larry.'

'This is foolproof, Grandpa.'

'How many times do I have to tell you not to call me Grandpa?'

Mao took off his rucksack and Willem noticed the slogan on the other boy's ever-present filthy T-shirt.

'Is the Shining Path a religion?' he asked.

'It's a sect,' I said. 'Haven't you heard of the Illuminati?'

'Where's the CD player?' Mao asked.

He was wearing a compact disc on the index finger of his right hand.

'What are you doing with that?' I asked him. 'I thought cockroaches were deaf?'

'Students have known about this poison since the seventies,' Mao announced. 'They discovered it by accident; sit-ins aren't the cleanest places in the world, as you can imagine, and it's the only remedy proven to keep roaches at bay.'

'But what is it? White noise?'

'Something much worse. Cuban ballads.'

He put the disc into the machine, turned the volume up as high as it would go and soon the chords of a guitar were joined by a tuneless voice singing: *At the end of this journey in life our bodies will be swollen from going to death, to hatred, to the edge of the sea* . . .

'Well, of course this'll work!' I yelled, trying to make myself heard above the music. 'I'll kill myself and the cockroaches won't bother me any more!'

At the second verse, the cockroaches in the kitchen stuck their antennae out and started scuttling about, bumping into the walls. They were promptly joined by the creatures in the bedroom and the bathroom.

'Open the door!' Mao shouted to Dorotea, who was nearest to the exit.

She did as she was told while the song continued with its torture: *We are the prehistory of the future, we are the distant annals of man . . .*

Hundreds of roaches were emerging from every corner of the apartment, hissing as they went, crashing into our shoes and then surrounding us as they headed for the living room. Dorotea hopped up onto the Corona chair, her long mane of hair standing on end in disgust and at the chords pulsing from the CD player; Willem, paler than usual, began to pray with his eyes shut.

'I told you!' Mao crowed.

'How does it work?' I asked. 'Is it something in the singer's voice? Is there a background noise in the recording?'

'Roaches are counter-revolutionaries!' Mao replied. 'Everyone knows they're biological weapons of the CIA!'

'And who does the CIA work for?' I yelled. 'God, or evolution?'

'It's true!' he insisted. 'They use them to spread epidemics!'

The moment the song finished, the apartment was free of pests, Dorotea was able to get down from her chair and Willem was restored to sight once more.

'Praise be to Gawd,' he said.

'That wasn't God,' Mao corrected him, 'that was Silvio Rodríguez.'

I went over to the stereo and pressed the stop button before the next song started up.

'What are you doing?' Mao cried. 'Do you want the roaches to come back?'

'Don't tell me I've got to have this music on all the time to keep them away?' I asked.

'Cockroaches have no memory,' he explained. 'If you turn off the music they'll come straight back.'

'Do you think I'm going to leave this CD playing all day long at this volume? Where do you think we are, Guantanamo?'

'In Guantanamo they play death metal, Grandpa. Leave it on for a while, just play a bit every day.'

I pressed play, the sound of the guitar and the voice returned and we started shouting again.

'I'm going to need something stronger in that case!' I yelled. 'What'll you have?'

'I should go!' Willem bellowed.

I was about to offer him a glass of water so he would stay, but Dorotea got there first and gave me another idea.

'I'm going to go and say hello to my grandmother while I'm here!' she said.

As I stood in the doorway and said goodbye to them, I winked my left eye at Willem, who responded by painting his transparent larva face bright red.

'I wanted to say sorry,' added Dorotea. 'I didn't think things would get so complicated.'

She smiled and I saw that her plump upper lip formed a crease beneath her nose: a second smile.

'And there's nothing you can do about it?'

'I don't work there any more, they fired me,' she replied sadly.

'Don't worry, I've got it all under control.'

'So they didn't reopen the case?'

'No, but I've got to compensate them instead.'

'Community service?'

'Something like that.'

Behind the couple, in the darkness of the corridor, the cockroaches crowded together in mounds in the corners.

'Can I do anything for you?' Dorotea asked.

'Such as?' I replied.

'I don't know, help you out with your shopping, take you to the doctor's, whatever you need. Can't I change this bulb for you? It's dangerous having it so dark in here, you might trip over something.'

I looked from the height of the crown of Dorotea's head to the position of the light: not even by standing on one chair on top of another would the tiny young woman manage such a feat.

'I've ahfered to do that far him severl times,' Willem interjected, who just had to stretch out his arm in order to touch the ceiling, 'but he doesn't want me to.'

'It's the responsibility of the management of the building,' I told them.

This was true: just as true as the fact that they ignored Francesca and that, deep down, the unreplaced bulb didn't really bother me, because darkness seemed to me a place conducive to mix-ups and offered me more possibilities of slinking away without being hassled by members of the literary salon.

'You should probably all leave,' I said. 'You're making my cockroaches nervous.'

'Anything you need, you let my grandmother know and I'll be here,' Dorotea insisted, before, protected by Willem, who was waving his Bible threateningly in his right hand, she turned to face the sea of cockroaches.

I closed the door and turned back to Mao, who had settled himself into my little armchair, his dreadlocks pulsing to the rhythm of the guitar.

'What's your poison?' I shouted.

'I'll have a beer!' he replied.

'By the way! Any news from Tlalnepantla?'

'Not yet, but my comrades from the TAC are looking into it as we speak!'

'The TAC? Terminal Anti-Christ Centre?'

'The Tlalnepantla Anarchist Collective!'

I opened a large bottle of supermarket own-brand beer, reserved for occasions such as this, and poured out a glass. I then took out my last bottle of whisky: of the five pints I'd acquired during my heroic excursion barely two remained, little more than a pint and a half, really. I held the glass out to Mao and when I was about to sit down in the Corona chair the intercom buzzed again. I looked around to see if Willem or Dorotea had left something behind. I couldn't see anything. The song came to an end and in the few seconds before the next track began, I picked up the receiver to hear Francesca shouting: 'Turn the volume down!'

I hung up and walked over to the balcony. A hysterical Francesca had already stationed herself outside on the pavement.

'We can't concentrate with that racket! Turn it down!'

'Give me my book back!'

'Turn the volume down or I'll report you to the building manager!'

'Give me my book back or I'll report you to the public prosecutor's office!'

At that moment, I saw Willem and Dorotea come out of the building, wait for a car to pass, cross the road and go into the Chinese restaurant together. I moved away from the balcony before Mao could come over. The intercom buzzed once, twice, an infinite number of times.

'I like your remedy more and more!' I told Mao.

'What was that about a book? Did someone steal a book of yours?' he asked.

'I lost a small battle with the salon and they're holding my copy of *Aesthetic Theory* hostage!'

The music persisted, stubbornly cramming too many syllables into each line, and there wasn't so much as a whisker of a cockroach in sight. Then I had an idea.

'Fancy earning some hard cash, Mao?'

'Want me to get you another copy of *Aesthetic Theory*? Go on, cheap as chips at twenty pesos.'

'You're pretty capitalist for a Maoist, aren't you?'

'You've got to put capital to work for the Revolution. I can get you a copy.'

'No! Mine's already underlined.'

'So what, then?'

'I've got a plan to get it back.'

'Just say the word, Grandpa.'

I started explaining the idea as it occurred to me, on the fly, and Mao perfected it, demonstrating some quite astonishing powers of military strategy. I offered him another beer, and another, and when the plan was fully fleshed out we agreed on a date and a fee, then I switched off the music to call the cockroaches back. Mao downed the rest of his beer and said he'd better go and look for Dorotea. On his way out, he saw the copy of *Notes to Literature* on the shelf by the door.

'Weren't you going to give that to someone?' he asked.

'There was a change of plan,' I replied. 'By the way, do you have access to the philosophy faculty library?'

'Yep. What do you need?'

'Bring me everything you can on literary theory.'

'Structuralism, hermeneutics, semiotics, reception theory?'

'Whatever, the more out-there the better.'

Just then someone banged at the door, and I geared myself up to confront Francesca, but it was a kid who'd been mugged and was asking for money to cover the bus fare to Pachuca. At least that was what he said, that was his sales pitch. He'd slipped into the building while Francesca was shouting at me. It was pure gold: if Francesca was planning on calling an extraordinary general meeting to report me for playing my music too loud, then I would have a counter-accusation ready.

'Does your mobile phone have a camera on it, Mao?'

'All phones have cameras, Grandpa.'

'Take a picture of my comrade here. Smile, kiddo.'

It wasn't me who ended up proving that a man could get used to anything, even the ignominy of giving a literary workshop in some godforsaken bar. Sundays came and went, and I'd even managed to get Papaya-Head to pay the tab, which meant that, if I managed to keep the classes going indefinitely, I'd get fifty-two additional days of life for every year – a whole extra year if I extended the classes for seven years! You could call this literally living off literature.

We began at around midday and ended, at the earliest, at half past five. Each week, I equipped myself with enough ammunition to start another argument and prolong the session for as long as I wanted, thus enjoying the resulting free drinks. The lack of civic-mindedness displayed by the students of the faculty of arts and humanities was of great help: every book was pertinently underlined. While Papaya-Head read the start of his novel aloud, in which he described, in maddening detail, the fur colour, the way of looking around, and the weight and the *texture* of the growls, among other trifles, of each and every one of the hundreds of dogs his protagonist hunted down, I flicked through the books on literary theory in search of some passage that would let me interrupt his reading and initiate a pointless discussion that would raise the tone and necessitate we move from beer to tequila.

'Stop there,' I would say, 'your readers have already fallen asleep. Worse: your readers have already died, they died in the nineteenth century! And I've got bad news for you: dead people don't buy books. Now pay attention.' And I read:

> *An analysis of literary history shows how empty spaces have moved from being elements of narrative economy or producers of tension and suspense – characterised by the figure of the ellipsis – to their central role in modern literature, with its fragmentary nature, in which, according to Wolfgang Iser, narrative forms of a segmented character allow for an increase in the number of empty spaces in such a way that the segments left blank become a permanent irritation in the reader's constitutive activity.*

'You see?' I asked him. 'You don't have to tell the readers everything, you can put lots of empty spaces in your novel.'

'But I don't want to irritate the reader!' he complained.

'Precisely! Put some empty spaces in! With any luck your novel will disappear completely!'

One day, a single phrase from *Notes to Literature* was enough to last us until the bar closed: *It is no longer possible to tell a story, but the form of the novel demands narration.*

'Well that's obvious!' objected Papaya-Head. 'It's not possible to do anything that way! If you're trying to put me off, or make me give up writing this novel, the deal's off. I'll cancel the workshop, reactivate the report against you, and Bob's your uncle.'

'You don't understand,' I replied. 'What this sentence means is that you have to write even though it's not possible any more, you see? What's important is trying. It's like sport: it's not winning that matters, it's how you play the game – get it? I'm going to need something stronger. Two mezcals!' I shouted at the barman, who was bustling about behind the bar.

As the afternoon went on, the regular customers would approach our table to amuse themselves with our discussions, which grew more antagonistic with each glass.

'What you want is for me to fail!' Papaya-Head said, accusingly. 'This must be the worst literary workshop in history!'

'I told you I didn't know how to write a novel!'

'So why did you agree to teach me?'

'Because you threatened me!'

'Saboteur!'

'Blackmailer!'

'Decrepit old sod!'

'Big fat papaya-head!'

Even so, the following Sunday we both turned up for the meeting: I, so he'd pay for my drinks; he, so that I'd read him some garbled theoretical passage that would keep his brain occupied during the week, and so gloss over his inability to write a novel.

He had appeared one night on the corner and stood there observing me for a while from the shadows, watching as I bustled about chopping the meat, warming up the tortillas, dishing up the food. Despite the state he was in, skinny as a skeleton, his eyes bulging, I had recognised him straight away. We'd spent many a night together, endless early mornings of excess and chaos. He looked like he was living on the streets, and he came surrounded by a sorry-looking pack of stray dogs. The dogs were malnourished, mangy, flea-ridden. They were dogs with parvovirus, with sores. Dogs that had lost all hope of being rescued, or had never had any. Dogs not even my mother, with her infinite affection for canines, would dare to bring back home. Looking at the group, it wasn't clear who was in worse company, him or his mutts.

I went over and held out a plate of tacos for him, before he could scare my customers away. I knew from the way he looked at me that he didn't remember me. He wolfed down two tacos and shared the rest out between the dogs, causing a brief scuffle punctuated by growls. Then he came over with the plate in his hand. I thought he wanted more tacos; charity is a bottomless dish, as I'd learned very quickly.

'I'll sell you a dog,' he said.

The other diners at my stand stopped chewing for a minute and threw him a curious, disdainful glance. One of the regulars said: 'What's going on? Don't tell me you're dealing with suppliers at this time of night?'

The others burst out laughing at the joke, and the dogs growled a reply. I gave the plate back to the Sorceror with more tacos on it, which he ignored.

'I'll sell you a dog,' he repeated.

'You've got the wrong stand, compadre,' I said, cutting him short. 'The guy with the *pozole* stand around the corner will buy it off you, for sure.'

The audience laughed again at the joke, it was an easy crowd, and the Sorcerer retreated into the shadows, where he waited for a while until he grew bored and moved off. The scene began to be repeated almost daily, although he had a habit of disappearing periodically. If I didn't have any customers I'd stand and talk to him, trying to grasp the thread of his ramblings. He spoke as if the Apocalypse had happened last week. He said he would have shown me his paintings but they'd been stolen. At other times he told me he'd had to pawn them then asked me for money to help get them back. I thought that in this state it was impossible he'd still be painting, that it was all part of his delirium, unless he'd stopped being a figurative painter and switched to abstractionism. He still didn't remember me, no matter how much I persevered.

'Don't you remember? We met in La Esmeralda.'

'I took three classes in La Esmeralda and they didn't teach me anything,' he replied.

'We met outside, you don't remember? On the corner where the whole gang would get together to go out drinking.'

'What did you do at La Esmeralda?' he asked.

'I took classes.'

'In what?'

'Life drawing.'

'Impossible. No such thing as an artistic taco seller.'

And over and over, he'd try again: 'I'll sell you a dog.'

When we were alone, I explained: 'These dogs are no good, my friend.'

'Which ones?' he asked.

'These ones!' I replied, indicating the sorry pack at his feet.

'Are you mad? These are my friends. I'm selling you *another* dog.'

'Another one? Which one?'

'I'll catch it, if you buy it. You can pay me in advance.'

And this was what our encounters were like, as nights came and went, until one of my regular customers, who lived in the same street as my stand, cracked one last, sad gag: 'What are you going to do now your best supplier's kicked the bucket?' he asked.

'What?' I asked, not understanding.

'That crazy dude who kept trying to sell you a dog. Didn't you hear? They found him a couple of blocks away, surrounded by dogs, face down in the street.'

The effects of the kidnap of my *Aesthetic Theory* were proving devastating: the telesales calls became tortuously protracted with no way of putting an end to them aside from hanging up, which only led to the phone ringing once more immediately and everything starting all over again. I had tried using the books on literary theory as a substitute, but they didn't work. Not because of the content, which was equally impenetrable, but in all likelihood because, deep down, I didn't trust them: a fetish allows no substitutes. The crisis reached such a peak I was even sent a loyalty card for a hardware shop and a box containing free samples of shampoo for taking part in a marketing survey. Juliet told me: 'This happens because you've got a telephone – why on earth do you have a phone line? All it does is make the richest man in the world even richer!'

'It's for emergencies,' I replied.

'Emergencies my foot! At our age any emergency is fatal and as far as I know, dead people can't use the telephone.'

'Steady on, *Juliette*.'

'I'm joking! You're so touchy. Why don't you leave the phone unplugged?'

'What if someone calls demanding a ransom for my *Aesthetic Theory*?'

'Don't be daft, Teo; all that drinking's drying up your brain.'

'Are you going to start lecturing me too?'

'Not likely. Want another beer?'

I spent my days in a state of agitation that sent me completely round the bend: I lost count of the drinks I had; I started shouting for the slightest reason, playing at killing cockroaches by throwing objects at them from a distance, and coming and going from the building without rhyme or reason. Willem noticed the change in me and thought I was concealing a different kind of sin: 'Are yuh takin' drugs?' he asked.

I shot him a filthy look and he persevered.

'If you're takin' drugs then you need help.'

'You want to help me? Then get my *Aesthetic Theory* back!'

'It's only a book.'

'You're wrong, Villem, it's much more than a book.'

'The Lard punishes devotion to material things.'

'Oh really! What if material things aren't material? Since when has a book been a material thing? What if it had been your Bible that had gone missing, you wouldn't be so calm then, eh?'

'If my Bible went missing it would be because it had to fawll into the hands of someone with more need of it. I would gert another Bible. Why don't yuh buy another copy of the book?'

'Because that would mean giving up, and I'm not going to do that. Francesca has to give me back my *Aesthetic Theory*.'

'Why are you fighting?'

'We're not fighting.'

'No?'

'No.'

'What are you doing then?'

'It's a mating ritual.'

Willem flushed.

'Speaking of mating, Dorotea sends her regards.'

'You saw Darotea?'

'No, but she left a message with *Juliette* and now here I am, acting as messenger between the two lovebirds.'

He put the Bible in his rucksack as if it would get dirtied by his thinking about a woman while holding it in his hands. He looked at his wristwatch and the little badge with his name on, which he had pinned to his shirt pocket, at the level of his heart, trembled.

'Have you been seeing her a lot?' I asked.

'A few times.'

'In the Chinese restaurant? It's a very romantic place.'

'And near the university.'

'And?'

'And what?'

'What do you mean, "what"? Don't tell me you trek all the way across the city to talk to her about the word of God.'

'We talk about lats of things, we have a lat in common.'

'Are you both as naive as each other?'

'She's a missionary too, in her own way.'

'Well, at least you agree on coital positions.'

'What?'

'Nothing, forget it. Watch out for that boyfriend of hers, mind – he's got guerrilla training.'

Since something didn't add up in this story, I went to see Juliet in the shop and together we analysed the state of the romance.

'I want you to promise me something, *Juliette*,' I said.

'That we can help plan the wedding?' she asked.

177

'That if you find out all of this is another one of Mao's operations, you'll tell me.'

'How could it be an operation? My Dorotea's not exactly Mata Hari.'

'Mao's got an endless supply of conspiracy theories. I only hope he hasn't got it into his head to use Dorotea to infiltrate the Mormons.'

'Why are you so worried? It's almost as if Villem was your son.'

'I like the boy, he just needs a bit of experience.'

'Does it turn you on, Teo?'

'Eh?'

'Don't play dumb with me. It turns you on to think of your little Mormon boy screwing my Dorotea. You're a pervert.'

It was three in the afternoon already and all we'd been given to eat was peanuts, crisps and two miserable little fried tacos with beans. Papaya-Head was resolutely reading the opening to his novel and drinking oh-so-slowly, hindering the steady flow of bar snacks. I was starving, so the next time he took a breath to signal the full stop, new line and space between one paragraph and the next, I interrupted him.

'Hurry up, the bar snacks are running out,' I ordered him.

'What?' he asked.

'Finish your beer and order another one so they'll bring us some more food.'

He downed what was left in his glass in one gulp and I ordered another large bottle, which came accompanied by two bowls of soup each the size of a ten-peso piece.

'Is that all?' I asked the waiter.

'Do you want more?' he replied. 'You're taking your time today.'

Twenty minutes later, we were in the same place: I, starving; Papaya-Head, absorbed in the meanderings of his novel.

'Hey, what did you have for breakfast?' I interrupted him.

'Sausages,' said Papaya-Head.

'Stands to reason.'

'What does?'

'You're trying to destroy me. Come on, drink up!'

'Oh, I'm destroying you, am I? You're not listening to me.'

'Of course I am, I don't have a choice.'

'Well you're not telling me how I can improve my novel.'

'Because it's all bad!'

'All of it? Tell me one thing that's bad, just one!'

'Just look at the protagonist, look at the things you say about him to justify his dog-killing. You say he's solitary, he's an alcoholic and a drug addict, a womaniser, that he's got a scar on his face and a toothpick in his mouth, like a ruffian from the movies. You paint such a bad picture of him it's as if you're trying to say that evil is a physical attribute.'

'It's based on a true story,' he said, defensively. 'It's a portrait of the owner of the butcher's shop who we caught selling dog meat. I've got the photos they took when they arrested him.'

'And you think that explains his behaviour?'

'His behaviour's explained by the fact that he's a frustrated guy who doesn't even want to be a butcher.'

'No shit! I'm going to let you in on a secret: no one wants to be a butcher, not even if they love it, except someone has to be a butcher, right? Otherwise the world would be full of poets, artists, actors and intrepid explorers, and the parks would be full of statues honouring them, but there'd be no one to make things work. Someone has to hunt the bison, sow the fields, turn the screws of the world. And in any case, you're judging your character without considering one fundamental detail.'

'What's that?' he asked.

'First finish your beer,' I ordered him, and I leaned back so he'd understand I wasn't going to continue until he did so.

He obeyed, I shouted at the waiters to bring us another large bottle and finally they sent over two plates of *pozole*.

'You've forgotten where your protagonist lives,' I told him, 'where he was born and grew up. Are you from Mexico City?'

'No, I'm from a little town in the provinces', he replied.

'I knew it! You don't understand this city. In your town they call a guy who kills a dog a dog-killer; here, they'd call him a survivor.'

'Actually, in my village they'd call him a cynic.'

'And here we call people like you provincial. Don't you get it? Dogs don't matter. It doesn't matter that they're dogs. They're dogs just because they are, but they could be anything else that worked as a symbol of life's cruelty. If they weren't dogs they'd be rats, or rabbits.'

'The dogs are dogs because this is what happened. The dogs matter because that's reality.'

'Reality doesn't matter.'

'Do you mind telling me what does matter, in that case?'

'I don't know, but I'll tell you one thing I know for sure doesn't: the fact that you're writing a novel.'

'All you want to do is ruin me.'

'All I want to do is eat *pozole* and it's getting cold – do you mind?'

He stood up, making a great show of pushing his chair back noisily.

'On your own head be it,' he warned me.

And then something happened that really did matter: Papaya-Head walked across the bar, angry as a bullet, and left without paying.

The voice on the telephone, a female voice all fuzzy with static that had asked to speak to me, identified itself by saying it was calling from the public health clinic in Manzanillo. My father had just died of cancer and someone had to deal with the body. I bluffed as best I could and Mum didn't ask any questions, even smiling at me, fancying that this mysterious phone call meant I was finally going to stop bumbling through life and start putting the story of my failed marriage to Marilín behind me, after all these years. When she went out to walk the dog, I told my sister what had happened.

'I'm not going,' she said.

'We promised him,' I replied.

'*You* promised him – I've already buried him, in a graveyard in Manzanillo, just like we told Mum we did, like normal people do. Or had you forgotten?'

I told my mother I was going away for a few days and she didn't ask where or with whom, only smiled again, even more broadly this time. My sister and I had become adults, but Mum hadn't stopped being Mum and she would only cease to be so if we made her a grandmother, something that would never happen.

I got on a bus and, fourteen hours later, arrived in Manzanillo. My father was waiting for me at the station. For a dead man, he looked dreadful (they might have put some make-up on him). For a living one, he looked like a ghost. I hugged his puny bones to me and gave him a loud telling-off, right into his ear to make sure he would hear me: 'You've got to stop doing this. What happens when you really die one day and I don't believe you and you end up in an unmarked grave or in the university's medical department?'

'That's what happens in children's stories and you're an adult now,' he replied. 'Where's your sister?'

'She wouldn't come, she says she's already buried you.'

'She promised!'

'I promised, and here I am. Don't tell me you want me to cremate you alive!'

He suggested we go and have lunch at a seafood shack by the sea, but I refused; I didn't want this to become a family tradition. We ate in a restaurant in town, which was unbearably hot in spite of the ceiling fans spinning round as quickly and as noisily as they could. When my father saw me fanning myself with the menu, he said:

'I told you: there's not a breath of air in here. We didn't have to suffer for nothing. You're just like your mother.'

'Didn't you have cancer?'

'I did, but I got better.'

'You don't say! So why did you make me come here, then?'

'Not so fast, all in good time. How's your wife? You got any kids?'

'I'm not married.'

'Weren't you going to get married?'

'Weren't you going to die?'

'So we've both been jilted. I hope your bride was prettier than mine – mine was frightful.'

The most uncomfortable thing was not the heat but the fact I didn't dare keep my gaze fixed on my father's face. Not, at least, without having the slippery sensation that his eyes were going to pop out of their sockets at any moment. We ate our prawn cocktail and octopus in silence, and then I tried to draw the encounter to a close.

'Why did you make me come?'

'I changed my mind. Or rather, I didn't change my mind, art changed its mind; art never stops. Painting is a thing of the past, I don't want to be cremated any more or have my ashes mixed with pigment. I don't want to go down in history as part of some anachronistic protest. I want my body to be used in a performance. Give it to Jodorowsky, let's see what he comes up with.'

'Jodorowsky doesn't live in Mexico any more, he moved to Paris.'

'Well give it to Felipe Ehrenberg, then.'

'I don't know him, I don't know anyone from that world any more, Papá; you took a long time to die, or rather, you're taking a long time.'

'If not Felipe then give it to one of the groups doing performances, happenings, there's loads of them, but look into it properly first, I don't want to end up in some frivolous puff of smoke.'

With his thin, skeletal fingers, he reached into his shirt pocket, took out a piece of paper folded in half and held it out to me. It was a letter of authorisation that declared he was 'in full use of his mental faculties' and wished to donate his body to art. It was a model letter: where it had said 'science' my father had crossed out the word and written 'art' over it. At the bottom, as well as his signature, were those of two witnesses and a notary's seal.

'When you come to collect my body,' he said, 'don't forget to bring this letter.'

The action lasted less than ten minutes and was carried out so efficiently I actually admired Mao's guerrilla training. Viva Peru! At the same time that Mao pressed the main doorbell and I pressed the intercom to buzz him in, I switched on the music on the portable CD player that Mao had brought over the day before. The cockroaches made for the exit and I cast them out, like a Pied Piper in reverse, towards the lift, which I'd jammed open with the Corona chair. The insects piled up in the lift, all on top of each other, making a mound, while from the speakers of the CD player came the words:

> *Yesterday I lost my blue unicorn,*
> *I left him grazing and he disappeared –*
> *Any information will be generously reimbursed.*

When the lift was completely full, I took the chair away and the doors slid closed: Mao had called it from downstairs. As soon as the lift completed its descent from the third floor, the wave of cockroaches spilled triumphantly out into the lobby. Terrified, the salon members fled as best they could out into the street. Mao pressed the lift button and it went back up to the third floor, carrying with it eleven little lights and eleven copies of *In Search of Lost Time*. We blocked the door open again with the folding chair and Mao lugged the *Lost Times*, three at a time, into my apartment.

Eventually, when all the *Lost Times* were inside we let the lift go and went back into the apartment; Mao, sweating; I, whistling the 'Ode to Joy'.

'A great triumph for the Revolution!' I exclaimed. 'Fancy a beer?'

'Sure, Grandpa – I haven't carried such hefty things since the Ibero-American Summit when a fat comrade of ours was wounded and I had to drag him for nearly two miles so the police couldn't catch him.'

I went to the fridge and took out a big bottle of Victoria I'd saved for this moment. Mao flopped down onto the little chair and began flexing his arms like he was warming up at the gym.

'What now?' he asked.

'Now we wait,' I said. 'Now the negotiations begin. Did they see you take the haul?'

'No, they ran out into the street and the cockroaches went after them. Didn't you see them from the balcony?'

'Yeah, they turned down Avenida Teodoro Flores and headed for the Jardín de Epicuro.'

As I poured two glasses of beer, the roaches started coming in under the door, at first timidly, the vanguard made up of four or five creatures, and then, brazenly, came the rest, the sheep, the cockroach-sheep.

'No way!' said Mao. 'Where are they coming from?'

'Cockroaches,' I told him, 'are an army with infinite reserves, like an endless nation of robots.'

'Shall we play them the music?'

'No, leave them be.'

'Hey, what are you going to do with those bricks?' he asked, pointing at the tower of *Lost Times.*

'I told you: negotiate the handover.'

'I need to borrow them off you.'

'So now you've got a literary salon. Didn't you tell me the novel was a bourgeois invention?'

'I don't want to read them. I've just had an idea.'

'Take them, I can't risk having them here for long in any case.'

I handed him a glass of beer and raised my own:

'To the Revolution!'

'No, to Revolutionary Literature.'

'Whatever.'

A long time had passed since Willem had buzzed at the main door and he still hadn't managed to get to the door to my apartment. Doubly mystified, because it wasn't even a Wednesday or a Saturday, I went out onto the balcony: nothing. I heard the intercom buzz again straight away.

'What's going on? Why don't you come up?' I asked.

'We have him,' said Francesca.

'Eh?'

'We have your little friend. We're not going to let him go until you give us back our *Lost Times*.'

'I don't have your *Lost Times*.'

'Don't lie, I know you planned it all with the help of that ragamuffin.'

'I don't know what you're talking about.'

'That kid who leaves our lobby stinking of sweaty feet.'

'I don't have your *Lost Times*, I've told you already.'

'I heard you. Either you give them back or we won't let your friend go.'

'Are you sure? Do you know what kidnapping a gringo could cost you?'

The pause at the other end of the line confirmed my threat was having the desired effect.

'I'm going to hang up, *Frrrancesca*, I have to make a call to the North American embassy.'

'On your own head be it,' she warned me.

I put the phone down and went and stood by the door to wait for Willem. He took only the five obligatory minutes and then appeared in the doorway with the face of a martyr mid-torture.

'My parents want me to come home,' he said.

'Come on in.'

He came in, his rucksack full of woe, or at least that's what it looked like: a rucksack that pushed his shoulders downwards, emphasising his dejection.

'A tequila, Villem?'

'A glass of wahder, please.'

'Did they scare you?'

'What?'

'They tried to kidnap you.'

'Eh?'

'What were you doing down there? Why did you take so long?'

'They wanted me to talk to them about the word of the Lard. I was reading my Bible to them far a while.'

I held out his glass under the water dispenser and, as I filled it up, I saw that, uncharacteristically, Willem had left his rucksack by the door and had sat down in the little chair without his Bible.

'What is it,' I asked, 'family problems?'

'My parents are afraid,' he replied. 'They say there's goin' to be a big earthquake.'

'How do they know? Did Jesus Christ tell them?'

'They saw the news.'

'What news?'

'The crack that's openin' up in the ground. They say it's a worning, that there's goin' to be a big earthquake any moment.'

I handed him a glass of water and pulled the Corona chair over to sit opposite him.

'That's got nothing to do with anything,' I said.

'What do you mean?' he asked.

'You can't predict earthquakes. And anyway, they already explained that crack, didn't you hear? The revolutionaries' moustaches?'

He took a few little sips of water and rested the glass on the seat, squeezing it between his legs so it didn't spill.

'That's a dumb lie nobody believes,' he said angrily, losing the peace of the Lord. 'They say they got that stary from a book. And Darotea told me it's not true.'

'Dorotea is Mao's girlfriend,' I replied, 'and he is the king of conspiracy theories. Don't pay any attention. How long were you planning on staying?'

'Two yeahs altogether.'

'Well?'

'Well what?'

'What are you going to do?'

'I don't want to go.'

I waited for him to continue, keeping an eye on the glass he was balancing between his legs.

'Darotea isn't Mao's girlfriend any more,' he said.

'Oh really! Let me guess . . . that's why you don't want to leave.'

He looked up and into my eyes and I felt almost proud he'd matured to the extent that he'd at least stopped blushing.

'If you're going to stay,' I said, 'let it be for the right reasons. Stay because you want to, don't stay because of Dorotea.'

'I do want to stay because I want to, and if I want to stay it's because of Darotea.'

'Have you slept with her yet?'

'Sex before marr – '

'Yeah, I know, I know,' I interrupted him. 'So are you going to stay to screw her or to marry her?'

He looked away and over towards the door, towards his rucksack, where his Bible lay, in which perhaps, I imagined he was thinking, on one of its hundreds of pages, was the answer.

'I should go,' he said.

He stood up resolutely and the water spilled all over his crotch. He caught the glass before it fell to the floor and began to brush at his trousers with his hand. I handed him a roll of toilet paper to dry himself with. The liquid spread a dark patch all across the fabric, now decorated with a pattern of little white spots, the remnants of the loo roll.

'Wait,' I said, and went to my room.

I knelt down to take out the box of Chinese fortune cookies and came back into the lounge. Willem had already slung his woe over his shoulder, and it looked even heavier now.

'Pick one,' I said.

He put his hand in doubtfully but without making a fuss, as he wasn't programmed to disobey anyone in any circumstances. He fished out the little parcel, unwrapped it and split open the cookie.

'And?'

'The helping hand you need is at the end of your orm.'

'Bingo!'

He put the scrap of paper in his shirt pocket, behind the badge with his name on, at the level of his heart.

'If you do leave, come and say goodbye,' I said.

'I'm not goin' to leave,' he replied.

'Good.'

I watched him go, weighed down with a determination that filled him with guilt. I shut the door and began imagining the scandal down in the lobby when they saw him walk past with his trousers in such a state.

No one gives out medals or erects statues to taco sellers, but a taco seller, especially a taco seller in the centre of Mexico City, can achieve recognition, too. I reached the height of fame in the eighties, when my taco stand in the Candelaria de los Patos was frequented by the cream of metropolitan society, not to mention the whey and the curds as well. One of my regular customers was the mayor: he came escorted by his minders, who also ate, taking turns so they never dropped their guard. Their most important job was stopping the other customers from coming over to the mayor with petitions that would end up giving him indigestion. Another customer who came at least once a week was El Negro Durazo, who back then was the chief of police in the capital, before we had a change of presidents and people realised, miraculously, that he was the Devil's envoy to Mexico City. He was not a customer I was proud of, but he was one of the most loyal. He stopped coming only when they tried to put him in prison and he had to flee.

Once José Luis Cuevas came; by then already an acclaimed artist, he was trawling the centre with Fernando Gamboa trying to find a site to build his museum. I was too embarrassed to tell him we'd met before, to ask him if he remembered me.

Another regular customer was Alberto Raurell, who was the director of the Museo Tamayo and had organised a Picasso exhibition. Even though he was half-gringo, or precisely because of this, he adored tacos. When he came to eat at my stand, I would pester him so much chatting to him that his tacos would grow cold and I'd have to keep serving him fresh ones. The coterie of daily diners – locals, office workers and night owls of all descriptions – would tease me: 'The taco guy fancies himself an art critic!'

And Raurell, smiling but serious, always came to my defence: 'This is what we need, taco sellers who are interested in art.'

I told him of my buried aspirations to be an artist, of my fleeting passage through La Esmeralda, said that I still went to museums, to galleries, but didn't think there was anything interesting to look at any more, that the great art from the first half of the century completely eclipsed that of the second half, and nothing really new was being made. Raurell didn't accept my views, he'd hold his taco with the fingers of his right hand intertwined, in that strange way of those who didn't learn how to do it as children, and started giving me lessons in aesthetic theory between mouthfuls, very patiently.

'Of course new art's being made,' he'd say again and again. 'New art's being made all the time. Do you know what a German *theorrrist* used to say? That the new is the desire for the new. You see? Imagine there's a child in front of a piano looking for a new tune, one that's never been played. This child is doomed to fail, to be frustrated, because this tune doesn't exist, all possible melodies have already been *considerrred* on the keyboard, due to the simple fact that a keyboard exists with a determinate combination of keys. You see? But the new is what the child does, he wants to make something new. The new is the desire for the new. The new is the child's stubbornness. This is the *parrradox* of art. You have to seek out the new. If you don't seek, you don't find.'

'What's his name?' I asked.

'Who?'

'The German guy who said that.'

'Theodor Adorno. Read Adorno, you'll like him.'

Before the crowd started ridiculing me again I got myself off the hook: 'When do you think I've got time to read, boss? I've got to work, you've no idea how lousy the life of a taco seller is.'

Raurell winked at me, raised his left hand, the right one busy trying to keep hold of the taco disintegrating between his fingers, and waved his index finger in the air as he spoke in a loud voice, so everyone could hear him: 'I've had better conversation about art at this taco stand than in Harvard, I swear!'

Later on, Raurell was killed; he was eating in a restaurant in the centre of town, not far from my stand, when there was an armed robbery; he put up a fight and they shot him. It was in all the newspapers. He was thirty-four years old. In the Museo Tamayo there was an exhibition on Matisse that he had curated, so colourful and joyous it seemed like a macabre joke. The following year they captured El Negro Durazo. He was accused of extortion, possession of illegal weapons, smuggling and corruption, and was sent to rot in jail. He was one customer I wasn't sad to lose.

The intercom buzzed as I laboured away at my notebook and drained the dregs of what until then I had thought would be the final beer of the day.

'I've come from the BDD,' said Mao's voice on the phone.

'Do you know what time it is?' I asked.

'It's an emergency.'

'Broken-hearted Drunks Delivery?'

'How did you guess?'

'The tone of your voice says it all. Did you get the whisky?'

'Not yet.'

'Have you got anything with you?'

'A couple of beers and a packet of peanuts.'

'Is that all?'

'And a joint.'

'Well, why didn't you say so before? Come on up.'

He arrived after the obligatory five minutes the lift took to complete its ascent, which gave me time to put the Cuban torture into action.

'The roaches will never leave at that volume,' Mao said as he came in.

'That doesn't matter,' I replied. 'Francesca's in her apartment now, supposedly sleeping, and I don't want her to hear us.'

'Aren't you being a little over the top?'

'Have you seen how thin these walls are?'

He handed me the two warm cans of beer to put in the fridge and took a little packet out of his pocket that contained, quite literally, three peanuts.

'I got hungry on the way,' he said apologetically.

'And the joint?' I asked.

He unzipped his rucksack then undid another zip inside the bag, and eventually extracted half a deformed, squashed little roll-up. As I took it from him I noticed it was warm.

'Did you fancy a quick toke on the way too?' I asked. 'Have you got a lighter? I haven't smoked for quite a while.'

'Yeah, I figured.'

'Really?'

'Just the way you hold the spliff, I've only ever seen that in a film about The Doors.'

I took the lighter from him and walked over to the fridge. Behind me, Mao had discovered the sketchbook I'd left open, carelessly, on the armchair. Out of the corner of my eye I saw he had started to flick through it, pausing, it seemed to me, at the drawings.

'Your pics are awesome,' he said. 'Do you only draw dogs and women? If you drew them together it'd be full-on perversion. You'd better watch out, you know, the last guy they caught with that fetish was accused of murdering Luis Donaldo Colosio. Remember the Eagle Knight? He had a sketchbook just like this.'

'Did the Maoists teach you how to snoop as well or are you just rude?'

'Hey, chill out, Grandpa, you're so touchy. You'd better not go writing anything about me, now.'

'As if – you're not exactly very interesting.'

'I'm serious, it'd put me in danger, and you too.'

From the depths of the fridge I rescued a can of Tecate beer I'd been saving since the day the lights went out for several hours. Then, from its hiding place, I took out the half-litre of whisky I had left.

'So Dorotea's left you, lover boy?' I said, to change the subject.

As I expected, he lost interest in the sketchbook, putting it down on the table, and switched to concentrating on his woes.

'You know about that?' he asked. 'Did the Mormon kid tell you?'

'And there I was thinking you were trying to infiltrate the Mormons.'

'Well, that was the idea.'

'And it really backfired, didn't it! You didn't reckon with our good friend Villem's charms, did you.'

'I'm gonna punch his lights out, that little fucking gringo son of a bitch.'

'Calm down, Mao, I thought you'd had a proper education.'

'You're offended by swear words, Grandpa? Well whaddya know.'

'I'm talking about your sentimental education. I thought you were made of sterner stuff.'

I passed him a can of beer and flopped down on the armchair with a glass of whisky in one hand and the joint, now lit, in the other. I raised my glass to make a toast.

'To mariachis everywhere,' I said.

'If you're going to take the piss I'm leaving,' he complained.

'Seriously, relax kiddo, sit down. The world doesn't end because of a woman, not even one like Dorotea. Didn't the

Maoists teach you anything about love? The next thing you know you'll end up risking the Revolution for it.'

'What the hell has love got to do with the Revolution?' he asked, dragging the Corona chair over to sit down next to me.

'It's got everything to do with it. A true combatant shouldn't have any ties. Have you ever, in the history of humanity, seen a real revolutionary with a wife and kids? Can you imagine a terrorist in love? Love makes you vulnerable, it makes you feel like you've got a lot to lose, it changes your priorities, takes away your freedom – want me to go on?'

He knocked back a long gulp of beer.

'It's flat.'

'Oh is it now! Unlucky for you.'

'And what was your Revolution? '68, the Tlatelolco Massacre? You never had a family – or did you?'

'In '68 I was thirty-three, kiddo – the only revolution I fought was giving tacos away to the students who showed up at my stand.'

'Seriously?'

'Just for a few days. Then word got around and I had to stop. You know what they say: charity is a bottomless dish.'

'So?'

'So what?'

'So why did you end up alone? There must have been a reason, no one ends up alone just because.'

'Go and ask people why they got married, why they had kids. The world is full of people who get married just because, get divorced and remarry just because – what's so strange about ending up alone just because?'

'Pass it on, will you?'

I handed him the diminutive joint and, as I was out of the habit, I burned his fingers.

'Sorry,' I said. 'Kill that reefer, buddy.'

'You sound like someone in a William Burroughs novel.'

'You've read Burroughs? I thought you didn't read.'

'An ex-girlfriend made me read it.'

He took a pair of tweezers from his rucksack and used them to hold the tip of the joint to finish what was left.

'So you're not going to tell me?' he asked.

'Tell you what?'

'Why you never married.'

'I've already told you.'

'Sure you're not a poof?'

'Yeah right, and now you're properly pissed and stoned I'm going to rape you.'

'So touchy. I'll bet there's a story behind it'.

'Why does there have to be a story behind it? Why does there always have to be a story that explains things? Since when does life need a narrator to go around justifying people's actions? I'm a person, not a character in a book, kiddo.'

'If you don't want to tell me don't, just stop talking bullshit. I liked you better before, when you just used to read Adorno. All those books on literary theory are frying your brain.'

'And I liked you better before too, when you used to walk like you were dancing to reggae; now you walk around jerking all over the place like a polka.'

The joint disappeared, literally, between the tweezers, and Mao leaned back in his chair to exhale, in one long puff, the last toke he'd managed to extract from it.

'How are the negotiations going, by the way?' he asked.

'We're just arranging a time and a place for the first round,' I replied.

'Got you.'

'Don't you go losing my *Lost Times*, now.'

'As if.'

'What are you going to use them for?'

'I can't tell you anything, it would jeopardise the operation.'

He drained the last of his beer, made a face, and got up. His Shining Path T-shirt looked even scruffier than usual, with thousands of stains of varying origins, an odd little hole near his belly button and the left sleeve unravelling, although it had perhaps been like this since day one and I was only noticing now because I was stoned.

'You're the least discreet Maoist I know,' I said to him. 'It's almost as if you want to be caught – is that it? You want them to catch you so you've got something to moan about?'

'Is it because of my T-shirt?' he replied. 'That's just to put people off the scent.'

'You mean you're not a Maoist?'

'Yeah right.'

'So why did you tell me you were?'

'I didn't, you reached that conclusion all by yourself.'

'*Juliette* told me.'

'Are you sure?'

'So you're not a Maoist?'

'Course I'm not.'

'So what are you?'

'That question doesn't matter any more, Grandpa, times have changed. We live in a post-ideological era, in case you hadn't noticed.'

'Post-ideological? Aren't you the one who keeps on going on about novels being a bourgeois invention?'

'That's not ideology, Grandpa, that's history.'

'So what's your real name, Mao?'

'That question doesn't matter either. And anyway, you're not really called Teo, either.'

'So you've never been to Peru.'

'The closest I've been to Peru is a restaurant in La Condesa where they do a mean ceviche. Speaking of which, has anyone ever told you you've got a nose like a potato?'

'Watch it, "Mao". And do you mind telling me, since I suppose you don't speak Chinese either, how you figured out that the guys in the Chinese restaurant over the road are Korean? Or did you make that all up?'

'I used the translator on my phone, Grandpa.'

He picked up his backpack and slung it over his shoulder, putting an end to the conversation and getting ready to leave.

'Now I'm hungry,' he said.

'That's a good symptom,' I told him.

'Of what?'

'That you're not going to die of a broken heart.'

'Or that that was some good quality ganja.'

'There's a taco stand on the corner that opens late.'

'Bleurgh, they look gross, they're probably made of dog meat.'

'No shit!'

The first round of negotiations took place one Saturday after-noon on neutral ground, chosen by Francesca: a Sanborns café opposite the Jardín de Epicuro. The mediation would be Juliet's responsibility, as she claimed to be an expert in these sorts of conflict.

'It won't be the first or the last time I've done it,' she had said, when she put herself forward as a candidate.

When Francesca, jealous, tried to allege favouritism towards my cause due to our being friends, Juliet interrupted her and defended herself:

'Madam,' she said, 'I take umbrage at the suggestion that I'll replicate the vices of the corrupt State.'

On the negotiating table there was a cup of tea, for Franc-esca, and two beers. First and foremost, I informed them that I wasn't prepared to drag out the discussions for ages.

'It's best we get straight to the point,' I said, 'the beer here cost me thirty pesos.'

'It's quite a simple negotiation,' Francesca replied. 'We'll be done in no time at all. You give us back the *Lost Times* and the reading lamps, and if you don't, I'll report you to the management committee.'

'I've already told you twenty times,' I replied, 'that I don't have the *Lost Times*. If you lost them, you need to look for them properly. You know what they say: he who doesn't seek doesn't find. Oh, and I don't have the reading lamps, either.'

'Well in that case I don't know what we're doing here,' said Francesca, looking at Juliet.

'Let me explain what the negotiation consists of,' I said. 'You give me back my *Aesthetic Theory* and I'll make a certain compromising photograph of you disappear, or else – '

'What are you talking about?' she interrupted.

'The photo of that lad you so carelessly let into the building. I'd love to know what the management committee thinks of its dictator infringing her own rules. I'm debating whether to ask you to resign.'

'I didn't let anyone in!'

'I don't have your *Lost Times*!'

'I don't have your *Aesthetic Theory*!'

'Now look here,' Juliet intervened, 'let's just calm down. I suggest we put together a hypothetical scenario to start the dialogue off. It's an imaginative exercise, all right, before you dismiss it out of hand.'

Francesca nodded and I took a tiny sip of beer, just to moisten my mouth.

'Let's imagine,' Juliet continued, 'that this lady has in her possession the copy of *Aesthetic Theory* belonging to this gentleman.'

'Even though I don't,' Francesca said.

'I told you, this is hypothetical,' Juliet said. 'Let me finish. And let's imagine also that the gentleman has the copies of *Lost Time* and the reading lamps that belong to the salon members. Better still: let's imagine something else. Let's imagine, instead, that you don't have the books, as you both insist, but that you might be able to obtain them, you understand? You don't have them, but, if a friendly agreement were reached, you could get hold of them. Based on this supposition, would you feel comfortable carrying out an exchange?'

'I can't give what I don't have,' I said.

'Nor can I,' Francesca said.

'But what you might be able to do is each indicate to the other where they could find what they're looking for. It would be an exchange of information.'

'I'll tell you what I can give to the gentleman,' Francesca declared.

She put her hand into her pocket and retrieved a folded piece of paper, which she handed to me.

'What's this?' I asked.

'Read it,' she replied.

It was a photocopy of a medical report stating that I was not 'legally competent' and 'not liable for prosecution' because I suffered from alcoholism and senility.

'This is a fake document!' I cried.

'It's an official document,' Francesca said. 'The Society for the Protection of Animals requested it and thanks to this certificate you were let off a fine. Do you know what would happen if I handed it over to the management committee? You know the rules very well: I could send you to an old people's home with this little piece of paper.'

In my head I saw Papaya-Head's papaya head and I imagined beating it to a pulp, or cutting it into little pieces with an enormous butcher's knife.

'This is an insult!' I shouted. 'I'm leaving the table. The negotiation's off.'

I left immediately, without waiting for an answer, mainly because I wasn't prepared, on top of everything else, to pay the bill. The following day, as was to be expected, Papaya-Head didn't show up to the literary workshop in the bar. On Monday, with the help of Juliet, who called Dorotea, I got hold of the man's telephone number. After downing two tequilas, I rang him with rage coursing through my veins.

'Traitor!' I shouted as soon as he answered the phone.

'Saboteur!'

'How you could stoop so low?'

'I could say exactly the same: all you ever wanted was to stop me writing my novel. You know that after just one session with Francesca I've already got the first chapter?'

'You betrayed me for a novel!'

'Go and find someone else to buy your drinks!'

'You big fat papaya-head!'

I heard him hang up and the mere prospect of ending up in an old people's home made me drink that day until I lost consciousness.

'Will you let me draw you?'

'Tomorrow.'

'Can I hold your hand?'

'Tomorrow. Weren't you going to look for another job?'

'Tomorrow. Can I kiss you?'

'Tomorrow. Didn't you say the taco stand was temporary? When are you going to stop selling tacos?'

'Tomorrow. Will you marry me?'

'Tomorrow. Why don't you enrol at university to study something useful?'

'Tomorrow. Will you let me come in and watch while you pose?'

'Does it turn you on, Teo?'

Wanks came and went, and thus, life went on.

Our bodies floated in a desert-like wilderness studded here and there with dead trees that looked as if they would come to life at any minute thanks to some wizardry; dead trees that, instead of growing green again, and covering themselves with leaves, threatened to pull their roots from the earth and start walking; dead trees with branches like arms, monsters from a child's nightmare; trees like the living dead. On the horizon a few rocky hills were visible and, up in the sky, some strange clouds, clouds whose shapes not even a meteorologist or an art critic would be able to decipher.

I squeezed my hands to calm Marilín down, because I sensed she was with me, but I wasn't squeezing anything at all, Marilín wasn't there. Instead, I could see the back of the Sorcerer, delicately moving his right arm, from which poured, in anguished brush strokes, the surrounding landscape. He finished painting a tree and floated over towards me holding his palette and his paintbrush. He started looking at the landscape as if looking at the landscape were an order: *look at the landscape!* he ordered me with his gaze, *look at the landscape!* I looked at the landscape and wished I wasn't there, in this prehuman apocalypse, as if life on Earth had ended before it had begun, as if evolution had gone wrong and life were slowly dying out without having managed to produce even a tadpole, as if the world were going to end and the only vestiges would be these sorrowful trees.

The Sorcerer breathed deeply, and I breathed deeply, and in that world there were no smells other than the greasy smell of oil paint.

'Where's Marilín?' I asked.

'Marilín, Marilín . . . ' he replied.

He stretched out his neck, his head passing through the physical bounds of the canvas, and when I imitated him I could see his bedroom. On the bed, tangled up in sweaty sheets, lay Marilín, her hands and feet tied, condemned by the tape over her mouth to an oppressed silence. On the walls were framed still lifes with fruit: peaches that were buttocks, watermelons and dragon fruit that were vaginas, and on the bedside table, a papaya cut in half obscenely displaying its gelatinous belly.

I put my head back inside the painting, propelled by a dizzying rage my hoary old body couldn't match. My fist waved slowly around in the static atmosphere of the apocalyptic landscape.

'Calm down, compadre, don't be like that,' the Sorcerer said.

'Let her go!' I shouted.

'That depends on you. If you fulfil your side of the bargain nothing will happen to her, I promise. I didn't want to go to such extremes, but you don't seem to understand.'

'What do you want me to do?'

'You still don't get it?'

'How can I if you haven't asked me to do anything?'

'Do I have to tell you? Are you going to waste the symbolic power of a dream and settle for literalism?'

'Or we could play a guessing game.'

'You're a bit slow, aren't you. Very slow, in fact.'

'Well?'

'Well what?'

'What is it that you want?'

'Do you really not understand? I want you to write a novel about me!'

'I don't write novels!'

'There you go again!'

'I wanted to be a painter, an artist; I was never interested in literature.'

'You *wanted* to be a painter, you *wanted* to be an artist, but you weren't.'

'And I'm not a writer, either!'

'But you've got an artistic temperament, which is what matters. When you have an artistic temperament you can use it equally for music or for painting or for literature. Let me show you something.'

Then the Sorcerer left his palette and paintbrush on the branch of a tree, which took them as if it had fingers, and put his hands in his trouser pocket, from where he was going to take out a fortune cookie. Curiously, I knew that it was a fortune cookie without having seen it, as if it were in my own pocket, and I could feel the Sorcerer's cadaverous fingers rummaging about near my groin, not his, and the shock and the tickly feeling made me wake up.

I was so drunk, still, that I decided I'd better not get up, although this was what my head was demanding: that I go to the toilet, wash my face, fetch a glass of water. Instead I stayed lying down with my eyes open, watching the darkness spinning around, and at a certain point, before I fell asleep again, I clearly heard the door to my apartment opening stealthily, and closing again a moment later. I stuck my arm out from under the sheets and reached out to turn on the main light. I held my breath to try and detect any sound coming from the lounge: nothing, just the cockroaches bustling about as usual. In my dozy state, I bent down and picked up the box of fortune cookies, to complete the dream. I tore off a wrapper, broke the cookie in two and unrolled the little piece of paper: *The future's not what it used to be.* I switched off the light and returned to my fitful sleep, the discomfort heightened by the cookie crumbs that had spread themselves all over the sheets.

In the morning when I remembered the sound of the door opening I began to investigate, as much as my headache allowed me, to see if anything was missing from the apartment. I found nothing. I took my daily pills and left the apartment intending to sort out my thoughts – and my hangover – at the greengrocer's.

In the lobby there was a dismal atmosphere: the salon members were staring at their hands and discussing, between sighs, a few chapters from *Lost Time* that they'd particularly enjoyed.

'So who died this time?' I inquired.

'Don't forget,' Francesca replied, 'you've got twenty-four hours.'

I went over to the greengrocer's without managing to dodge the sun, which sent twinges of pain through my forehead that nearly made me vomit. I had never been so thankful for the gloom and the cool air of the shop's back room. When she heard me stumbling in, Juliet looked up from her newspaper.

'Did you see?' she said, referring to what she'd been reading in the paper. 'They've evacuated over a mile of land around the Monument; they're saying the crack is spreading.'

'Can you give me something to drink?' I begged.

'You look a right mess, Teo. I can smell you from here.'

'Can I have a beer or not?'

'All right, mister, calm down, you can have a beer, you know you can, but I think you need to eat something, too. Shall I get us a couple of tacos? My stomach's rumbling now, too.'

I agreed, gave her a twenty-peso note and collapsed onto a chair next to where Juliet had been sitting – she was now walking to the front of the shop to shout out our order for tacos and beer. She returned, spread the newspaper open on the table and sat back down.

'I already feel like I'm in a bar with you just from breathing in.'

'Francesca came into my apartment last night.'

'Did she try and rape you?'

'Hey, I'm being serious.'

'What, your hangover's so bad you can't even clown around any more?'

'I don't feel like clowning around.'

'Let me get you a painkiller.'

'I've already taken something.'

'How do you know Francesca tried to get in? Did you see her?'

'I didn't see her, but I heard the door opening and closing. I was half asleep, I couldn't get up.'

'Perhaps if you didn't drink so much . . . '

'If I didn't drink so much Francesca wouldn't have come into my apartment?'

'If you didn't drink so much you would have got up and caught her red-handed. Supposing she did come in, that is. You're being paranoid, why would she want to come in?'

'To look for the *Lost Times*.'

'She could have done that before. She doesn't need to now, she's got you by the you-know-whats.'

'That's a bit of an exaggeration, *Juliette*.'

'No it's not, it's true.'

'By the way, did you talk to Dorotea?'

'She promised me she'd give him the message.'

'I asked you to get hold of Mao's phone number!'

'She wouldn't give it to me, she said it was for our own safety.'

'Those kids really like playing games, don't they!'

'What, and you don't?'

A boy entered the shop carrying two paper plates of tacos and a large bottle of beer.

'Hang on,' Juliet said, 'don't eat them yet, I'm going to give you a Serrano chilli to make you feel better.'

She poured out two glasses of beer and held out the chilli after rubbing it between her hands to make it even more savage. Then we ate in silence. She chewed and chewed and I chewed and sweated, drenched from head to foot. The beer performed the miracle of returning me to a state far more comfortable than that of being hung-over: drunk. Juliet brought me a roll of toilet paper so I could wipe the sweat from my face and blow what was starting to drip out of my potato-nose. As I blew, it occurred to me I'd never asked Juliet – who, when you thought about it, was an expert in such things – if it were true my nose had the form of a tuber.

'Hey, tell me what my nose looks like.'

'You really want to know? You're in such a mood today . . . '

'Is it a potato?'

'Yeah, but a Peruvian potato, you know what I mean, those dark-skinned ones.'

I passed her my glass for more beer and as she took it she looked at me, as if trying to calculate the size and nature of my need.

'Why don't you have a lie-down?' she suggested. 'A little nap would do you good right now.'

'Sleeping's the last thing I want to do,' I replied. 'I've been having some really weird dreams lately.'

'Erotic dreams?'

'I'm being serious, for God's sake! Why does everything have to be a joke?'

'Because you and I always joke around and, forgive me for saying so, but if it's jokes we're talking about then you're the king of jokes. Now, if you want to be serious, be serious: go ahead, tell me about your dreams.'

'I don't want to tell you my dreams, you might start trying to interpret them.'

'It'd be your fault if I did.'

'Oh would it now!'

'Of course, for giving me that trippy book.'

'Have you been reading it?'

'Bits of it, before I go to sleep; it's like a horror film. Wait a minute.'

I watched her as she walked across the patio and went into her room, returning shortly afterwards leafing through the book as she looked for a particular passage. She stood in front of me, turned a few pages over and eventually said:

'Here it is. Listen to this.'

And she read:

> *In us is also a dark angel (Hekate was also called angelos), a consciousness (and she was called phosphoros) that shines in the dark . . . This part has an a priori connection with the underworld through sniffing dogs and bitchery, dark moons, ghosts, garbage and poisons.*

She turned a page and then another one, and another, trying to find another bit to read out to me.

'Doesn't it give you nightmares?' I asked.

'Not on your nelly: I dream of Coatlicue every single night.'

Mao came into the bar dragging behind him the wheelie suitcase he'd taken the *Lost Times* away in. It was almost 8 p.m. and I'd lost count of how many drinks I'd had some time ago, out of sheer anxiety: so far from my *Aesthetic Theory* and so close to the old people's home. He sat down opposite me and starting flexing his right arm, the one he'd used to pull the delivery with.

'Damn it Mao,' I said. 'It was urgent. Didn't Dorotea give you the message?'

'We carried the operation out as soon as we could yesterday,' he replied. 'We had to bring it forward because of all the pressure you were putting on me.'

'And?'

'Complete success.'

'I'm talking about the *Lost Times*, I couldn't care less about your operations; do you have them?'

'They're in the suitcase. Can I have a beer?'

'Get your own beer, kiddo.'

He called to the barman to bring him a Victoria and stared intently at me; so desperate was he to tell me what had happened it looked as if the words were going to start tumbling out of his mouth like little balls.

'You really don't want me to tell you?' he asked.

'I thought it was a clandestine operation.'

'You helped the cause, you deserve to know.'

'You've got it all wrong, I don't have causes, I have problems; since we last saw each other things have got really complicated.'

I must have looked so downcast I imagined he even felt sorry for me, his dreadlocks drooping and depressed.

'Is there anything I can help you with?' he asked.

'For now,' I said, ' you can just wait here with me until the salon members go to bed so we can take the *Lost Times* up to my apartment. Then you can help me return them.'

'Whatever you say, Grandpa.'

We drank two or three more beers while I focused on stemming Mao's verbal diarrhoea as he stubbornly tried to make me an accomplice to his mischief, and then I sent him to have a look at the lobby. He came back and said:

'All clear.'

Back in my apartment, I opened the suitcase to check its contents and there were the *Lost Times*, all battered: the corners of the covers were bent, the pages looked wonky and some were loose and, stamped onto the cover of one, the print of a shoe was clearly visible.

'My God, Mao, what did you do?'

'I thought you didn't want me to tell you?'

'I don't want you to tell me a thing, but why are they in such a state?'

'We used them as weapons in the operation, Grandpa.'

'What operation? The Battle of the *Lost Times*?'

'Shall I tell you or not?'

'Tell me the minimum, I'm in enough trouble as it is.'

'The minimum is that we kidnapped a dog.'

'A dog?'

'Not just any dog: it belongs to the son of the richest man in the world.'

'Didn't that dog die?'

'They had another one: the Labrador's little lady-friend. We're going to demand the ransom in a few days.'

'I told you I don't want to know anything. Now, let's go to the Jardín de Epicuro.'

The next day, Juliet communicated the conditions of the handover to Francesca. The paper I found in my letterbox informed me that the *Aesthetic Theory* was in my apartment, under the bed. I found it stuffed into the box where I kept the Chinese fortune cookies. Meanwhile, the salonists rescued their *Lost Times* from the bushes in the Jardín de Epicuro. As their withdrawal symptoms had reached crisis point, they sat down immediately to read on the park benches. And that was where the police arrested them: using the battered books as evidence, they accused them of possession of weapons used in an attempted murder and unlawful deprivation of canine liberty.

The dog had been scratching non-stop at the door to my room, which meant that Mum had left the house without taking him with her. I hated this dog more than any other, even more than the dog that had made my father leave home, more, even, than Turnup, and before he became the definitive symbol of calamity. This dog was a nervous hound, who looked like he was about to have a heart attack even when he was asleep: he'd kick out his legs, tremble, bark and whine at oneiric enemies. My mother had named him Eighty-Three, the year she'd adopted him, because when she'd brought him home a couple of weeks after the demise of the previous animal, my sister had said that the different periods in our lives were marked by Mum's various mutts. It was true: when we recalled episodes from our past, we didn't say, that was in the sixties or in the forties, never mind 'before or after Dad left', which was the real watershed in the family history. Instead, perhaps to evade the issue, we said: that was when we had Turnup. Or when we had Market, that silky-haired dog who – in my defence, I would like to clarify – had ended up dying of a urinary infection that spread through his entire body and left him swollen like a balloon (and culinarily useless).

Eighty-Three had become an anachronism a year later, in '84, and by the time he was scratching at the door to my room, well into '85, he was a dead weight that tested my patience and made me doubt seriously whether the dog would live to see '86.

Around that time I used to sleep, or try to sleep, until midday, because I went to bed at 3 a.m. at the earliest, after closing the stall at midnight or at one on weekends, after cleaning and getting rid of the rubbish, pushing the cart over to a carport where I paid a guy to keep it safe for me, and having one or two drinks, which sometimes ended up being three or four, or five, in one of the nearby bars. My sister left for work early, and Mum came and went, running errands to fill the day like anyone with time on their hands does. Dogs had come and gone, and life had gone by: I was fifty years old and my sister fifty-one. After my father left, no one had been brave enough to leave home.

I got out of bed when my hangover let me remember that that morning, my mother was going to go to one of the few places she couldn't take the dog: the doctor's. The mutt wasn't going to leave me in peace until I took him out to have a wee. I went to the kitchen to get a glass of water and on the table I found the results of the tests my mother had been given the day before, a diagnosis that said, contrary to her belief, Mum was not suffering from any kind of heart condition. She'd left the results in the house on purpose, so the second opinion she was going to ask for today wouldn't be influenced by them. That is, so they wouldn't tell her she was a hypochondriac and send her home without doing more tests.

It was almost eleven o'clock, so I put on yesterday's clothes and, with Eighty-Three at my heels, went out into the communal passageway, where I discovered all my neighbours, every single one of them, gathered in groups that formed and then dispersed again, their radios playing at full blast, the doors to their houses open, the TVs on. My bewilderment lasted a second and then turned to astonishment when I saw Marilín walking towards me. As grudges had come and gone, we hadn't said a word to each other for twenty-five years.

Considering her legendary talent for flirting, something very serious must have happened: her face was bare and she wore a blouse and trouser get-up that could easily have been pyjamas. Without make-up, the wrinkles on her face were the proof of everything I hadn't wanted to see until then and which, as a matter of fact, I still didn't want to see.

'Where's your mother?' she asked me.

'At the doctor's,' I replied. 'What's happened?'

'Didn't you hear? There was an earthquake!'

'I was asleep.'

'I've been knocking at your door all morning.'

'I didn't hear. I'm a heavy sleeper.'

'Perhaps if you didn't drink so much . . . '

'If I didn't drink so much there wouldn't have been an earthquake? Really?'

'Where did your mum go?'

'To the doctor's.'

'Where?'

'I don't know, cardiology, I think.'

'Are you sure?'

'I don't know, I don't know, I think so.'

'They're saying the hospital collapsed.'

'Who is?'

'I don't know, on the radio, or the TV.'

'I'm going to talk to my sister.'

'Where is she?'

'At work.'

'The phones aren't working.'

I left Marilín and went back into the house without worrying about Eighty-Three, who came after me anyway, panicking now and with good reason, infected by the collective hysteria. I switched on the TV and then I saw the piece of paper on top with a message.

> *Don't forget I'm going to cardiology today. I don't know how long I'll be, so take Eighty-Three out to do his business. If I've got something serious and they have to keep me in, don't forget to feed him this evening. Your sister's coming with me.*

I showed up at the police station, accompanied by Dorotea and Willem, and we made a statement that the *Lost Times* had been lost the day the crime was committed and that the literary salon had only just recovered them when they were arrested. I brought along the money to cover the bail, an amount equivalent to two years of life. It didn't pain me to do so, not at that moment: five or six years more, instead of seven or eight, or three or four, seemed the same. And in any case, there was always the possibility of getting the bail money back if the salon members were acquitted. Less likely was that they'd be given back the *Lost Times*, which had become evidence in a criminal case.

We waited for the salonists to be released and when they came out there were no embraces or scenes of relief, only an exchange of glances halfway between hatred and gratitude, if a sentiment exists that can link the two. We'd come in a taxi and, since there was quite a gaggle of us now, I suggested we take the metro back. One of the salon members, one who throughout this whole story hadn't said or done anything to distinguish himself, said that he used to work around here and would be able to show us the way to the metro station. We set off in silence, Dorotea and Willem holding hands, me calculating how soon I could bust out a joke so it wouldn't feel so much like a funeral procession. I waited for two blocks, then I said: 'We really missed you guys.'

'Why did you do it?' Francesca asked.

Why did I do what, I thought? Loan out the *Lost Times* to commit a crime and then return them covered in evidence that would incriminate them, or pretend I knew nothing and say it had all been a mix-up?

'Why did I do what?' I asked out loud.

'Pay our bail,' she replied. 'You didn't have to, we were getting a collection together already. I'll pay you what I owe . . . '

'Don't get the wrong idea, *Francesca*, I didn't do it for the reason you think I did.'

'And what reason is that?'

'That I've gone soft, that I feel guilty, that I think I owe you all something.'

'And you don't?'

'Of course not.'

'Well then?'

'It's a negotiation. The real negotiation. You make that medical certificate disappear and I won't inform the management committee that their president is being investigated for a crime.'

'A crime of which I'm innocent.'

'That's why I paid the bail.'

'Because you feel guilty.'

'Because if the *Lost Times* hadn't disappeared none of this would have happened.'

'I didn't know you had a sense of justice.'

'Come and have a glass of whisky with me tonight and I'll explain everything I know about justice and executions, starting with the catacombs of the Roman Empire.'

'You pervert.'

'That's how I like it.'

We carried on walking in silence. It was that time in the afternoon when all that remained of the sun was the heat rising from the tarmac. I looked towards the horizon, through the buildings, and then I saw the self-portrait printed on a plastic sheet hanging from the wall of an old colonial building.

'STOP!' I yelled.

Everyone stopped dead, envisaging some imminent danger: a runaway car, a rabid dog.

'What is it?' Willem asked.

'What is it?' Francesca asked.

'What is it?' Dorotea asked.

'What is it?' the chorus of salon members asked.

I read out the advert for the exhibition: *Wounded Life: Manuel González Serrano (1917–1960)*.

'It's him,' I replied.

'Who?' Willem asked.

'The Sorcerer.'

I dragged the anonymous salonist who'd showed us the way over by the arm and, pinching him to prove I wasn't dreaming, I asked:

'What's your name?'

'Virgilio.'

And then one day, as was to be expected, as was normal, Dad really did die. A woman from the Manzanillo Forensic Medical Service explained it to me over the phone and, though it seemed more than likely to be true upon calculating my father's age, I wasn't prepared to fall into the same old trap again. I assured her I needed the death certificate so I could fill in some forms before I headed up there, and they faxed it over, to the stationer's outside the building I'd moved to and now lived in, alone. The ironies of life: before Dad's real death, I'd lived through the disappearance of my mother and my sister. The fax had come through all blurry, the image smudged and out of focus, but I made out the emblem of the local government of Colima and half my father's name. A half-truth, for the moment, that obliged me to confirm it.

I got on a bus and twelve hours later arrived in Manzanillo. At the station no one was waiting for me. I headed for the morgue to discover that my father really was dead and that he'd killed himself. He had taken cyanide, as well as a preserving formula that supposedly delayed the onset of decay in the body. He explained this in a note he'd left for me, the suicide note. In red ink and cramped, shaky letters leaning so far to the right that the words looked like they'd beaten him to dying, my father's message took me hours to decipher, sitting in the waiting room of the morgue as I waited for the body to be released.

The time has come. It's perfect. Take me with you to Mexico City and give me to SEMEFO. The art collective, mind you, not the actual forensic medical service. I saw a fantastic exhibition they put on in Colima last week: there were jars of human blood and drawings of corpses. Talk to Teresa Margolles, she'll think of something.

That same night I managed to cremate his body, and the next day I paid a fisherman to take me out to sea. When we were far enough away from the coast, I delivered my father's ashes to the Pacific Ocean.

'Who was he?' the fisherman asked me.

'My father,' I replied.

The man moved to the rhythm of the rocking boat, man and boat synchronised through the solitary routine of fishing. I closed my eyes to try and recall my father when he was young, but the only thing that came into my head was the image of a glass with a beer logo on that he used to rinse his paintbrushes in, the water forever murky. The fisherman interrupted my musings:

'Don't look now.'

Naturally, I opened my eyes and looked down at the surface of the ocean: a shoal of fish was devouring my father's remains.

'Do you mind?' asked the fisherman.

He was unfurling a net.

I told him I didn't.

And he began to fish.

Standing in front of the paintings in the exhibition, flanked by Willem and Dorotea, who had stayed to keep me company, I started to read the texts accompanying the pictures hanging on the walls: little pinches that were nonetheless failing to wake me up.

> *Born in Lagos de Moreno, Jalisco, in 1917, Manuel González Serrano belonged to the* Other Side of the Mexican School of Painting, *also known as* La Contracorriente. *His most prolific period was during the 1940s and the first half of the 1950s and, after a life characterised by numerous stays in psychiatric hospitals, he died homeless, on the streets in the centre of Mexico City.*

The museum was filled with an agitated buzz because it was about to close, and every room overflowed with the usual affluence: haughty old ladies with no discernment who didn't miss a single show, school children copying the titles of the works into their sketchbooks to prove to their teachers they'd come, groups of retired people ticking off an activity on the weekly agenda, foreign tourists hungry for their dose of exoticism and predisposed to misinterpretation, young couples who would go to eat an ice cream together afterwards. I slipped through the crowds grouped in front of the paintings, more concerned with getting to the next text, as if they were the last chapter in a book where the meaning of history, the meaning of my life, would be explained.

> *As a result of his near-total exclusion from public museographical archives, curatorial guides to temporary exhibitions and the literature on Mexican painting from the first half of the twentieth century, the Sorceror remains largely unknown.*

Dorotea and Willem could see how troubled I was and they followed me, asking over and over: 'Are you ok?'

'Do yuh want me to gert you a glass of wahder?'

And I said: 'Look, Villem, read this.'

And he read: *Once he had settled in the capital during the first half of the 1930s, he soon left his sporadic studies as an unregistered student at San Carlos and La Esmeralda.*

'And what does that mean?' Willem asked.

'Sporadic means occasional, from time to time,' I replied.

'Not that. I mean what does it all mean, the exhibition, everything. Does it mean everyone gerts to be remembered? That histary corrects its mistakes?'

'I don't know, Villem, this isn't a novel, this is real life, it's not that simple to explain.'

We left the museum when the guards threw us out and we began to walk – I staggered – following the instructions Virgilio had given us, towards the metro station. On the way, both my hands squeezed the exhibition guide, which I'd brought with me to prove, the next day, and the next one and the next, that this had really happened. We walked in silence, broken every now and again by the loud smacking kisses the two lovebirds were bestowing on each other.

The throng was visible two blocks away: the station appeared to be shut. In the crowd we found the salon members debating the best way to get back to our building.

'What's going on?' we asked.

'The metro's shut,' Hipólita informed us.

'The whole metro,' Francesca added. 'They say the city's in total chaos.'

We started eavesdropping on the conversations going on here and there, until we had a compendium of rumours. People said that the earth had split and the crack in the Monument to the Revolution had spread, criss-crossing the entire length of Avenida Insurgentes and Paseo de la Reforma. They said that a crowd had gathered around the statue, at first to gossip, but that things then edged closer to an uprising. They said that the Monument to the Revolution had collapsed. That the metro was closed for safety and would not be opening soon.

'I know how to walk back,' Virgilio assured us, and we set off, following him.

It took us almost an hour, at the doleful pace imposed upon us by the women's varicose veins, the men's bunions, several people's palpitations and everyone's shortness of breath. We witnessed a traffic jam, spanning the entire city, that was impossible to avoid save for abandoning one's car. We saw people pouring out into the street and we heard the subterranean clamour of something waking up.

When we got to our building, around 8 p.m., there were three lorries collecting rotten tomatoes from the greengrocer's. Juliet came out and called to me:

'The day has come, Teo, the day has come!'

Willem took me aside and spoke discreetly, his little name badge trembling next to his heart:

'Can I barrow your aportment?'

I gave him the keys and watched him cross the lobby, holding tight to Dorotea's hand, and couldn't help but feel a tingle go through me: history was about to write a glorious chapter. The door closed and I was left standing outside on the pavement.

'Are you coming?' Juliet asked, as she got ready to shut the shop.

'Where to?' I replied.

'People are gathering in the Plaza de la Ciudadela.'

'I'm too old for that sort of thing, *Juliette*, I'm going to have a beer.'

She gave a happy laugh and for a moment it seemed to me that the Revolution for her was one big carnival where she would be queen, but she was laughing about something else.

'You really are a pervert, Teo,' she said.

'Why?'

'What do you mean, why?' she said, looking down at my groin, 'just look, you've got your trousers wet already.'

I walked over to the bar on the corner, went in and headed straight for the toilets to scrub at my clothes with a bit of wet loo roll. Once I'd achieved the effect of making it look like I'd wet myself, I went and asked for a beer and a tequila then sat down in time to see Mao, who was dragging the suitcase the *Lost Times* had gone away and come back in, swerving madly over towards my table.

'Where's Dorotea?' he shouted.

'You're missing the Revolution, kiddo,' I told him.

'Tell me where she is!'

'You know where – she's with Villem.'

'I'm gonna smash that little Mormon's face in!'

'Relax, Mao, remember what we talked about the other day.'

He collapsed onto the seat opposite me, defeated, but starting to delude himself that this defeat was not, in fact, the one that mattered. It made me want to pat him on the back.

'Get me a beer, will you?' he asked.

I yelled to the barman to bring us another beer and a tequila each. The drinks arrived and Mao took a long swig of beer.

'We let the dog go,' he said.

'I told you, I don't want to know anything about that; the less I know, the better. The salonists are free for the time being, let's not make matters any more complicated.'

'I just want you to know we aborted the operation.'

'Fine,' I said.

I pointed with my chin at the suitcase we'd used for transporting the *Lost Times*.

'Did you get them?'

'I had to buy them. The first lot I just took out of the library and made them disappear. I would've had to trek round all the humanities departments in the country to get this many copies. Next time, let me know in advance.'

'How much?'

'One thousand one hundred pesos.'

'What?'

'A hundred each. But don't worry, Grandpa, I took the money out of the operation's budget.'

'That's good, because I wasn't going to pay you!'

He bent down towards the suitcase and started to unzip it, saying: 'I brought you something else, too.'

'The complete works of Adorno?'

'The elixir of Tlalnepantla,' he said, placing a bottle of whisky on the table.

'How much?'

'Fifty pesos.'

'Hey, I used to get it for thirty.'

'There's a twenty-peso anarchist tax.'

He carried on drinking his beer and tequila in silence, getting ready to turn the page, or to go back, as is still possible when one is young, to a time before Dorotea from where he could nudge history towards a different course. He emerged from his reverie with a dreamy look on his face.

'Did you hear about the plane?' he asked.

I told him I hadn't, and he passed me his phone so I could read the news in the paper: a terrorist cell had hijacked a plane full of stockbrokers travelling from London to New York using five copies of the annotated edition – all one thousand and forty hardbacked pages of it – of James Joyce's *Ulysses*.

'Our methods are spreading.'

He finished his drinks and said goodbye, telling me his comrades were waiting for him in La Plaza de la Ciudadela. I shook his hand and, before he left, I said:

'How can I reach you to let you know when I've finished the whisky?'

He wrote a mobile number on a serviette.

'When you call,' he said, 'ask for Juan.'

'You're called Juan?'

'No, that's the code.'

I ordered another beer and another tequila, then another, and another, until, just as the bar was about to close, Willem appeared with a smile so wide it made me realise I'd never noticed how huge his teeth were before.

'Well?' I enquired.

'*Ah'm* in love,' he replied.

'Tell me you used a condom.'

'Condoms are a sin.'

'Help me take this suitcase up to my apartment. And you're going to have to wash my sheets.'

They had to send the diggers into the rubble of the cardiology ward: they hadn't rescued my mother, they hadn't rescued my sister. Nor had they found their bodies, as with the thousands of others across the city. People began organising symbolic funerals, without bodies, without the dead. What was being buried, if anything, and not even this, was memories, nothing more.

A few weeks earlier, in one of her customary outbursts of hypochondria, my mother had given us instructions to bury her in the family tomb, in the Dolores public cemetery, half a mile from the Rotunda of Illustrious Persons. With her parents and siblings dead, all I had to do was get a letter of agreement from a few distant cousins whom we never saw and who didn't even bother coming to see her buried.

In preparation for the ceremony, I gave a nylon stocking to Eighty-Three, an incredibly long stocking, as long as my sister's legs, a stocking she would never wear again, and the dog's bones – inside a pine coffin with a little gold plaque with the names of my mother and my sister carved onto it – ended up on top of my Grandfather's, who had died in the Revolution, killed by a stray bullet.

The salon finished reading the first volume of *In Search of Lost Time* and to celebrate, they organised a cocktail party with champagne from Zacatecas and savoury crackers spread with tuna mayonnaise.

When I crossed the lobby on my way to the bar and they invited me to stay, I called out:

'All this sophistication plays havoc with my digestion!'

And just when it seemed that nothing else could happen, what with all the things that *had* happened, it turned out that the new delivery boy had been telling the truth. We only found out the night Hipólita tripped over the lost tin of jalapeño peppers on the first-floor landing. The management committee declared the boy innocent of theft and guilty of murder in multiple degrees: Hipólita didn't survive the fall. The salonists said: 'It's the supermarket's fault for having hired that negligent delivery boy.'

'It's the delivery boy's fault for not realising he'd dropped the tin in the corridor.'

'It's the management committee's fault for not properly maintaining the building.'

'It's the doctor's fault for giving her such a strong painkiller: it made her dizzy.'

'It's the plaster cast's fault: if she'd been able to put her hands down she wouldn't have hit her head.'

'It's her husband's fault: if he hadn't cheated on her she wouldn't have had to leave Veracruz and end up in this building.'

'It's the champagne's fault: it was too strong.'

'It's Hipólita's fault for having drunk three glasses of it.'

I tried to join in: 'It's Proust's fault, for not making *Lost Time* shorter!'

At A&E they told us she was stuffed full of painkillers. At least she hadn't felt anything. There was no funeral and no burial, because her children had the body cremated and took the ashes to Veracruz. They said they were going to spread them at the foot of the Pico de Orizaba volcano. Instead of a funeral procession, the whole salon organised a protest march to the supermarket. Juliet, who was a soppy old thing, presented them with a hundred pounds of tomatoes. When I saw them all troop by from my balcony I called out: 'There's a bookshop in the Alliance Française on Calle Sócrates!'

In an attempt to understand everything that had happened, I wrote in my notebook: *How can everything that's happened be understood? What's the meaning of it taking place? Was it a vindication of the forgotten, the disappeared, the damned, the marginal, the stray dogs? Was it a complicated way of saying art historians are revisionists? Was it a laboured joke that life played to rid itself of Hipólita? Or did Fate orchestrate it all to bring Willem and Dorotea together? What if they have a baby? What if the child ends up being the result of this whole story? Was it perhaps life that finds a way at any price? Or, worse, was there some sort of moral lesson that meant I'd have to give up drinking and channel my compulsions towards some other activity, such as writing a novel, for instance?*

The need to understand everything, to try and sum it up like a lesson, gave me uneasy dreams. Towards dawn, at the end of a corridor in a large exhibition space, I recognised the unmistakeable silhouette of the Sorcerer. I walked over and saw the Sorcerer do the same, surrounded by the usual pack of melancholy mutts.

'Now you really are ready to write my novel,' he said.

'Congratulations,' I replied.

'What for?'

'For the exhibition.'

'Do you think I'm interested in being recognised by posterity?'

'You're not?'

'I've suffered more than Christ; nothing can remedy that.'

'Nor can a novel.'

'You're right, but the novel you're going to write is *about* me, not *for* me.'

'So who's it for, then?'

'Who do you think? Look.'

And then he lifted up his shirt and, from down his trousers, where he had stuffed it, took a copy of *Aesthetic Theory*. He opened it up without hesitation at page 30, and ordered: 'Read this.'

And I read a phrase that stood out in golden letters: *The new is akin to death.*

'Am I going to die?' I asked him.

'Not yet,' he replied. 'First you're going to write a novel. Now wake up.'

'What?'

'WAKE UP, DAMN IT!'

I woke in a cold sweat, with a stabbing pain in my liver, and got up to get a glass of water and find a pill that would calm me. As I crossed the darkness of the lounge I saw a little light burning. I felt for the light switch and the bulb illuminated Francesca, clad in a long robe of red silk and sitting in my little chair, using the Chinese reading light to read my notebook.

'Give me the keys,' I demanded.

She waved a heavy bunch.

'My keys,' I insisted.

'I can't,' she replied. 'It's my responsibility, the responsibility of the chair of the management committee. Who do you think opens the door when someone here dies?'

'Have you been coming into my apartment this whole time?'

She fell silent, conceding that this was indeed what she'd been doing.

'But how is it possible I've only realised just now?' I asked aloud, although it sounded more like an expression of surprise bouncing around in my own head.

'You're a deep sleeper. Perhaps if you didn't drink so much . . . '

'If I didn't drink so much you wouldn't sneak into my room to spy on my notebook?'

She stood up and put the notebook down where her soft, firm, long-yearned-for posterior had been.

'Now you really are ready to write the novel,' she said.

'What?'

'I said now you can start writing the novel.'

'There's something I don't understand,' I said.

'What's that?'

'Why so insistent? What for, what do you get out of it?'

'You don't know? I work for literature.'

'You're kidding! Does it pay you a grant?'

'Something like that.'

'*Something like that?* What does *something like that* mean? You can't just come into my apartment and start playing guessing games!'

'What I get out of it is a novel.'

'You're not going to tell me you're a muse.'

She was silent again so as to confirm my suspicion and I raised my eyebrows just enough to demand an explanation.

'What did you expect?' she answered. 'A nymph flitting about by a river? A translucent young girl with long blonde hair and blue eyes sitting in a café in Paris? A dark-skinned beauty with huge breasts suckling the children of the earth?'

'For a muse you're certainly pretty twisted.'

'And don't forget I've got that medical certificate; if you carry on acting up I'll send you to the care home.'

'I thought muses were meant to inspire, not blackmail.'

'This is real life, not literature. And don't act dumb, all you ever wanted to do was go to bed with me.'

'Well?'

'Well what?'

'Is that going to happen?'

She put both hands to her waist, to the silk tie that served as a belt for the robe, and gently pulled at the knot, so gently that, instead of a no, the gesture had the vague air of a promise.

'We'll see,' she replied. 'First, write the novel. Write about us. Everything that happened to us. Write our story.'

I showed her the door with a matador's flourish and watched her go, propelled by her customary smugness and leaving behind her a faint scent of lemons. So I was going to have to write a novel. Francesca didn't know who she was dealing with. The next day I summoned Mao to an emergency meeting and, using the techniques he had learned for seizing public buildings, we installed a system for blocking the door to my apartment. That night I poured myself the last beer of the day, which turned out to be the third one before the second-to-last, and started to think about a novel whose author doesn't want to write it, a novel about something no one is sure has happened, a novel about what hasn't been experienced and, it goes without saying, a novel that would be like a plate of dog-meat tacos. I began flicking through the *Aesthetic Theory* at random, rereading the underlined passages, taking them as an inspiration, and then I opened my notebook, picked up my pen and started to write: *In those days, as I left my apartment each morning, number 3-C, I would bump into my neighbour from 3-D in the hall, who had got it into her head that I was writing a novel. My neighbour was called Francesca, and I, it goes without saying, was not writing a novel at all.*

AUTHOR'S ACKNOWLEDGEMENTS

To the members of the ICL, the Intimate Circle of Readers, whose evaluations significantly improved the manuscript of this novel: Andreia Moroni, Teresa García Díaz, Cristina Bartolomé, Rosalind Harvey, Iván Díaz Sancho, Javier Villa and Luis Alfonso Villalobos.

In some imprecise period of adolescence, in between sips of tequila, Óscar Serrano talked to me for the first time about his great uncle, Manuel González Serrano.

Patrick Charpenel was generous enough to give me a masterclass in twentieth-century Mexican art via Skype. Any inaccuracies there might be in this book are the responsibility of the novelist's brain.

Between sips of red wine and Barça goals, Manuel Silva tirelessly repeated to me that it wasn't possible to write, reflect upon art or even to breathe if one hadn't read Adorno's *Aesthetic Theory*.

It was Carmen Cáliz who, in her course on mythology at the Autonomous University of Barcelona, introduced me to James Hillman's excellent and disquieting (and totally trippy) oeuvre.

The (lightly edited) text from the exhibition on Manuel González Serrano come from articles published in *La Jornada* by Argelia Castillo and Alondra Flores Soto.

María Elena González Noval was the curator of the exhibition *La naturaleza herida* (Wounded Nature), first shown at Mexico City's Museo Mural Diego Rivera in 2013.

Some of the characters in this novel are real; most are fictional. Some of the events described are real; most are fictional. The dogs are all fictional: not one was killed in the making of this novel.

TRANSLATOR'S ACKNOWLEDGEMENTS

Rosalind Harvey would like to thank the Emerging Translators Network for help with elusive quotes and several thorny issues.

Dear readers,

We rely on subscriptions from people like you to tell these other stories – the types of stories most publishers consider too risky to take on.

Our subscribers don't just make the books physically happen. They also help us approach booksellers, because we can demonstrate that our books already have readers and fans. And they give us the security to publish in line with our values, which are collaborative, imaginative and 'shamelessly literary'.

All of our subscribers:

- receive a first-edition copy of each of the books they subscribe to
- are thanked by name at the end of these books
- are warmly invited to contribute to our plans and choice of future books

BECOME A SUBSCRIBER, OR GIVE A SUBSCRIPTION TO A FRIEND

Visit andotherstories.org/subscribe to become part of an alternative approach to publishing.

Subscriptions are:

£20 for two books per year

£35 for four books per year

£50 for six books per year

OTHER WAYS TO GET INVOLVED

If you'd like to know about upcoming events and reading groups (our foreign-language reading groups help us choose books to publish, for example) you can:

- join the mailing list at: andotherstories.org/join-us
- follow us on Twitter: @andothertweets
- join us on Facebook: facebook.com/AndOtherStoriesBooks
- follow our blog: Ampersand

This book was made possible thanks to the support of:

Aaron McEnery · Abigail Dawson · Abigail Miller · Ada Gokay · Adam Butler · Adam Lenson · Ajay Sharma · Alan Ramsey · Alana Marquis-Farncombe · Alasdair Thomson · Alastair Dickson · Alastair Gillespie · Alastair Laing · Alastair Maude · Alex Gregory · Alex Martin · Alex Ramsey · Alexandra Citron · Alexandra de Verseg-Roesch · Ali Conway · Ali Smith · Alice Nightingale · Alison Hughes · Alison Layland · Allison Graham · Allyson Dowling · Alyse Ceirante · Alyson Coombes · Amanda · Amanda Dalton · Amelia Ashton · Amelia Dowe · Amine Hamadache · Amy Rushton · Anderson Tepper · Andrew Lees · Andrew Marston · Andrew McAlpine · Andrew McCafferty · Andrew McCallum · Andrew Reece · Andrew Rego · Andy Madeley · Angela Creed · Angela Everitt · Angus Walker · Anna Milsom · Anna Vinegrad · Anna-Karin Palm · Annalise Pippard · Anne Carus · Anne Marsella · Anne Williams · Anne Claire Le Reste · Anne Marie Jackson · Annie McDermott · Anonymous · Anonymous · Anonymous · Anthony Carrick · Antonia Lloyd-Jones · Antonio de Swift · Antony Pearce · Aoife Boyd · Archie

Davies · Asako Serizawa · Asher Norris · Audrey Mash · Ayca Turkoglu · Barbara Anderson · Barbara Devlin · Barbara Mellor · Barbara Robinson · Barry Hall · Bartolomiej Tyszka · Belinda Farrell · Ben Schofield · Ben Thornton · Benjamin Judge · Bernard Devaney · Bernice Kenniston · Beth Mcintosh · Bianca Jackson · Bianca Winter · Bob Richmond-Watson · Brenda Sully · Brendan McIntyre · Briallen Hopper · Brigita Ptackova · Bruno Angelucci · Caitriona Lally · Calum Colley · Candida Lacey · Carl Emery · Carole Hogan · Caroline Perry · Caroline Smith · Cassidy Hughes · Catherine Edwards · Catherine Taylor · Cecilia Rossi & Iain Robinson · Cecily Maude · Charles Bell · Charles Lambert · Charlotte Holtam · Charlotte Ryland · Charlotte Whittle · Charlotte Murrie & Stephen Charles · Chia Foon Yeow · China Miéville · Chloe Schwartz · Chris Day · Chris Holmes · Chris Stevenson · Chris Elcock · Christina Moutsou · Christine Carlisle · Christine Luker · Christopher Allen · Christopher Jackson · Christopher Terry · Ciara Ní Riain · Claire Brooksby · Claire Fuller · Claire Williams ·

Clarissa Botsford · Claudio Guerri · Clifford Posner · Clive Bellingham · Colin Burrow · Colin Matthews · Courtney Lilly · Craig Barney · Dan Pope · Daniel Arnold · Daniel Carpenter · Daniel Coxon · Daniel Gallimore · Daniel Gillespie · Daniel Hahn · Daniel Kennedy · Daniel Lipscombe · Daniel Rice · Daniel Venn · Daniela Steierberg · Dave Lander · Dave Rigby · Dave Young · Davi Rocha · David Gould · David Hebblethwaite · David Hedges · David Higgins · David Johnson-Davies · David Johnstone · David Jones · David Roberts · David Shriver · David Smith · Debbie Kinsey · Deborah Bygrave · Deborah Jacob · Denise Jones · Denise Muir · Diana Fox Carney · Duncan Ranslem · Ed Owles · Elaine Rassaby · Eleanor Maier · Elie Howe · Eliza O'Toole · Elizabeth Bryer · Elizabeth Heighway · Elsbeth Julie Watering · Emile Bojesen · Emily Gray · Emily Jeremiah · Emily McLean-Inglis · Emily Taylor · Emily Williams · Emily Yaewon Lee & Gregory Limpens · Emma Bielecki · Emma Hewitt · Emma Perry · Emma Teale · Emma Timpany · Emma Yearwood · Emma Louise Grove · Eric E Rubeo · Erif Rison · Eva Tobler-Zumstein ·

Ewan Tant · Fawzia Kane · Finbarr Farragher · Finnuala Butler · Fiona Graham · Fiona Quinn · Fran Sanderson · Frances Hazelton · Francis Taylor · Francisco Vilhena · Friederike Knabe · G R J Beaton · Gabrielle Crockatt · Gabrielle Turner · Gary Dickson · Gavin Collins · Gawain Espley · Gemma Tipton · Genevra Richardson · Geoff Thrower · Geoffrey Cohen · Geoffrey Urland · George McCaig · George Savona · George Wilkinson · George Quentin Baker · George Sandison & Daniela Laterza · Georgia Mill · Georgia Panteli · Gerard Mehigan · Gerry Craddock · Gill Boag-Munroe · Gill Ord · Gordon Cameron · Graham R Foster · Hannah Jones · Hannah Perrett · Hans Lazda · Harriet Mossop · Heather Fielding · Helen Asquith · Helen Bailey · Helen Collins · Helen Jones · Helen Weir · Helen Wormald · Helen Brady · Helene Walters-Steinberg · Henriette Heise · Henrike Laehnemann · Henry Wall · Ian Holding · Ian McMillan · Ignês Sodré · Ingrid Olsen · Irene Mansfield · Isabella Garment · Isabella Weibrecht · Isobel Staniland · J Collins · Jack Brown · Jack McNamara · Jacqueline Haskell · Jacqueline Taylor · Jacqueline Lademann · James Attlee · James Cubbon · James Kinsley · James Portlock · James Scudamore · James Tierney · James Warner · James Wilper · Jamie Richards · Jamie Walsh · Jan Prichard Cohen · Jane Keeley · Jane Whiteley · Jane Woollard · Janet Mullarney · Janet Sarbanes · Janette Ryan · Jasmine Gideon · JC Sutcliffe · Jean-Jacques Regouffre · Jeff Collins · Jen Hamilton-Emery · Jennifer Higgins · Jennifer O'Brien · Jenny Newton · Jeremy Faulk · Jeremy Weinstock · Jess Conway · Jess Howard-Armitage · Jessica Hopkins · Jessica Schouela · Jethro Soutar · Jillian Jones · Jim Boucherat · Jo Harding · Joanna Flower · Joanna Luloff · Joel Love · Johan Forsell · Johanna Eliasson · Johannes Georg Zipp · John Conway · John Gent · John Hartley · John Hodgson · John Kelly · John Royley · John Steigerwald · John & Helen Milfull · Jon Lindsay Miles · Jonathan Watkiss · Joseph Cooney · Joshua Davis · JP Sanders · Judith Blair · Judith McLelland · Judith Virginia Moffatt · Julia Rochester · Julia Thum · Julian Duplain · Julian Lomas · Julie Gibson · Julie Van Pelt · Kaarina Hollo · Kapka Kassabova · Karen Davison · Katarina Trodden · Kate Beswick · Kate Cooper · Kate Gardner · Kate Griffin · Katharina Liehr · Katharine Freeman · Katharine Nurse · Katharine Robbins · Katherine El-Salahi · Katherine Green · Katherine Skala · Katherine Sotejeff-Wilson · Katherine Wootton-Joyce · Kathryn Edwards · Kathryn Lewis · Katie Brown · Katrina Thomas · Kay Pluke · Keith Walker · Kent McKernan · Kevin Winter · Kiera Vaclavik · Kimberli Drain · KL Ee · Kristin Djuve · Lana Selby · Lara Touitou · Laura Batatota · Laura Clarke · Laura Lea · Laura Willett · Laura Drew · Lauren Ellemore · Lauren McCormick · Laurence Laluyaux · Leanne Bass · Leigh Vorhies · Leonie Schwab · Leri Price · Lesley Lawn · Lesley Watters · Linda Walz · Lindsay Brammer · Lindsey Ford · Linnea Frank · Liz Clifford · Lizzie Broadbent · Loretta Platts · Lorna Bleach · Lottie Smith · Louise Bongiovanni · Luc Verstraete · Lucia Rotheray · Lucy Caldwell · Lucy Webster · Luke Healey · Lynn Martin · Lynn Schneider · M Manfre · Madeleine Kleinwort · Madeline Teevan · Maeve Lambe · Maggie Livesey · Mandy Boles · Mandy Wight · Margaret Begg · Margaret Davis · Margaret Jull Costa · Maria Pelletta · Marina Castledine · Mark Ainsbury · Mark Cripps · Mark Lumley · Mark Waters · Martha Gifford · Martha Nicholson · Martin Brampton · Martin Vosyka · Martin Price · Mary Nash · Mary Wang · Matt & Owen

Davies · Matthew
Francis · Matthew
Geden · Matthew Haley
· Matthew O'Dwyer ·
Matthew Smith ·
Matthew Thomas ·
Maureen McDermott ·
Meaghan Delahunt ·
Megan Wittling ·
Melissa Beck · Melissa
da Silveira Serpa ·
Melissa Quignon-Finch ·
Melvin Davis · Merima
Jahic · Michael Aguilar ·
Michael Holtmann ·
Michael Johnston ·
Michael Moran ·
Michelle Bailat-Jones ·
Michelle Dyrness · Milo
Waterfield · Mimi
Sanderson · Miranda
Persaud · Miranda
Petruska · Mitchell
Albert · Molly Ashby ·
Monica Hileman ·
Monika Olsen · Morgan
Lyons · Najiba · Nan
Haberman · Nasser
Hashmi · Natalie Smith
· Nathalie Adams ·
Nathan Rostron · Neil
Griffiths · Neil Pretty ·
Nia Emlyn-Jones · Nick
Sidwell · Nick James ·
Nick Nelson & Rachel
Eley · Nicola Hart ·
Nicola Hughes · Nicole
Matteini · Nienke
Pruiksma · Nina
Alexandersen · Nuala
Watt · Octavia Kingsley ·
Olivia Payne · Paige
Donner · Pamela Ritchie
· Pat Crowe · Patrick
Owen · Paul Bailey ·
Paul Brand · Paul
Griffiths · Paul Jones ·
Paul Munday · Paul
Myatt · Paul Robinson ·
Paul M. Cray · Paula
Edwards · Paula
McGrath · Penelope
Hewett Brown · Peter
Armstrong · Peter
McCambridge · Peter
Rowland · Peter Vos ·

Philip Warren · Phyllis
Reeve · Piet Van
Bockstal · PM Goodman
· PRAH Recordings · R &
A S Bromley · Rachael
MacFarlane · Rachael
Williams · Rachel
Lasserson · Rachel
Matheson · Rachel Van
Riel · Rachel Watkins ·
Read MAW Books ·
Rebecca Braun ·
Rebecca Moss · Rebecca
Rosenthal · Rebekah
Hughes · Rhiannon
Armstrong · Rhodri
Jones · Richard Ellis ·
Richard Jackson ·
Richard Major · Richard
Priest · Richard Soundy
· Richard Hoey & Helen
Crump · Rishi Dastidar ·
Rob Jefferson-Brown ·
Robert Gillett · Robin
Patterson · Robin Taylor
· Roderick Lauder · Ros
Finlay · Ros Schwartz ·
Rosalia Rodriguez-
Garcia · Rose Skelton ·
Roz Simpson · Rupert
Walz · Ruth Diver · SJ
Bradley · SJ Naudé ·
Sabine Griffiths · Sacha
Craddock · Sally Baker ·
Sam Cunningham · Sam
Gordon · Sam Ruddock ·
Samantha Sabbarton-
Wright · Samantha
Smith · Sandra de
Monte · Sandra Hall ·
Sara C Hancock · Sarah
Benson · Sarah Butler ·
Sarah Duguid · Sarah
Lippek · Sarah Pybus ·
Sarah Salmon · Sasha
Dugdale · Sean Malone ·
Sean McGivern · Seini
O'Connor · Sheridan
Marshall · Shirley
Harwood · Simon
Armstrong · Simon
James · Simona
Constantin · Simone
Van Dop & Tom Rutter ·
Sinead Reil · Sioned
Puw Rowlands · SJ

Nevin · Sjón · Sonia
McLintock · Sonia
Overall · Stefanie May
IV · Steph Morris ·
Stephanie Brada ·
Stephen Bass · Stephen
Karakassidis · Stephen
Pearsall · Stephen
Walker · Stephen H
Oakey · Steven Norton ·
Steven Reid · Steven
Sidley · Sue & Ed Aldred
· Sue Eaglen & Colin
Crewdson · Susan
Higson · Susan
Tomaselli · Susie
Roberson · Suzanne
Ross · Swannee Welsh ·
Tammi Owens · Tammy
Harman · Tammy
Watchorn · Tania
Hershman · Tara
Cheesman · Terry
Kurgan · Thami Fahmy ·
Thomas Bell · Thomas
Fritz · Thomas Mitchell
· Thomas JD Gray · Tien
Do · Tim Jackson · Tim
Theroux · Tim Warren ·
Timothy Harris · Tina
Rotherham-Winqvist ·
Todd Greenwood · Tom
Bowden · Tom Darby ·
Tom Franklin · Tom
Mandall · Tony Bastow ·
Tony & Joy Molyneaux ·
Torna Russell-Hills ·
Tracy Northup · Trevor
Lewis · Trevor Wald · UA
Phillips · Val Challen ·
Vanessa Jackson ·
Vanessa Nolan · Vasco
Dones · Victoria Adams
· Victoria Anderson ·
Victoria Walker ·
Virginia Weir · Visaly
Muthusamy · Warren
Cohen · Wendy
Langridge · Wenna Price
· Will Herbert · Will
Huxter · William Powell
· William G Dennehy ·
Zac Palmer · Zoë Brasier
· Anonymous

Current & Upcoming Books